DELI-DETECTIVE WRAPS IT UP

A Deli-licious Portobello Road Whodunnit

Glynn Christian

ISBN number (for paperback ONLY): 978-1-9162984-7-7

Cover design by Kevin Baldwin

Hendon Books London:
glynnchristian@hotmail.com

All love ends in heartbreak

From: The Inheritance
by Matthew Lopez, Old Vic, 2018

Quoted in A Previous Life
by Edmund White (Bloomsbury)

PART ONE

INGREDIENTS

•

August to November 1978

Chapter 1

•

Sunday, November 5th, 1978

Guy Fawkes Night. Bonfire Night if you don't do English history.

As ever, it means I'm catering at some rich customer's house. This time it's one of the cream-painted mansions that line Elgin Crescent, W11, which is north and down the hill from Notting Hill Gate and then curves to the west of Portobello Road. Most homes here are single-family and like this one those on the south side have gardens that open into a private park.

Onto bright Habitat plates piled high on the inevitable scrubbed pine table, candle-lit of course, the family and guests help themselves to my deli-kitchen's food. The famed deep-dish pizza. Long bread rolls with hot, sliced Polish mazurska sausage, salted cucumber and a smear of Moutarde de Meaux, that fashionable one with seeds and a red-wax seal. Black bean and pork-hock soup. An amaretti-biscuit cheesecake. Mulled wine from a preserving pan edged over the low element of an Aga range in new black.

The pyramid bonfire in the backyard is topped with a Guy Fawkes dummy hasn't long been lit, delayed because a busybody thought dead leaves should be raked further away and a few overhanging branches pulled off. That hadn't been appreciated because everyone had to come inside and then brave the garden a second time.

It is bloody cold out there.

Does no-one else think it curious still to be burning an effigy of the man who tried to blow up the Houses of Parliament in 1605? Really? Over three and a half centuries ago? Not a subject to raise when I am being paid to be there, I suppose.Once the fire takes, there is an amble out, bellies fuller, brains more wine-fuddled and enthusiastic sparklers streaming from gloved hands. Soon, there will be skyrockets.

Suddenly the chatter cools, leaving just the fire's cracks.

'Why is it bloody steaming?' someone shouts, sounding frightened.

Jem, the bony teenage son in charge of lighting fireworks directs his torch, creating a swirling aurora. High in the middle of the blazing fire the dummy's clothes are not even scorched. Instead, the stuffed figure is the centre of a churning column of steam. Unable to imagine an explanation, the guests giggle and clap their hostess.

'Meredith, you're so clever.'

Then the fedora slips, taking with it something that reflects the flames as it falls.

'Oh my God,' yells a woman from the blackness on the other side of the garden gate.

'That's my Freddy!'

Meredith is first to vomit.

I hope she'll pay for what is now staining her limestone paving. The richer they are, the more likely

Notting Hillbillies are to blame my food for any difficulties.

And the less likely they are to pay.

Saturday November 11th, 1978

Don't talk to me about sore feet, not until you've slapped cream cheese and smoked salmon into split bagels at 6am and then sliced, served and smiled in a deli until 6pm.

Like over-heated irons anyway, my feet pulse like steam pumps when I sit down for a break. If I get one. That's the reality of running a deli on Portobello Road on a Saturday.

Did I say? It's mine, Dan's Deli – A Farmer's Market Every Day of the Week. I'd only seen Farmer's Markets in New York but the description makes sense to my customers because I am pioneering the direct sourcing of artisan produce. Others - sausages and pates and cheesecakes - are made in my kitchen in the basement. My years of hippie trailing around Europe and the States taught me heaps before Brits knew they were keen on good food.

And me? Well, like a fair few around here, I'm the ghost of a 60s' hippie. That's not a look that takes long because ironing is optional. A beard speeds things, too. It's trimmed and tidy and this is where the grey hairs first popped. Grey amongst the blonde. Most of the time you can't see them there, or in my hair. I still wear that long. Shoulder stroking but sometimes in a ponytail caught low on the nape. I know, it's more a younger thing but I get away with it in these parts and I also get away with 30 on a good day. 30-ish, anyway. Add another decade for accuracy.

Good bone structure. Straight nose I think is like Clark Kent/Superman's in DC comic books. Generous lips, wide shoulders, narrow hips. Dark gold-brown eyes, said to have an appealing softness.

The 60s' chains and scarfs have gone, as have the silver rings, anything tie-died and the purple-lensed granny specs. The silver bangles and plaited wrist-bands stay. Sandals were never my thing. It's always been boots. Sometimes jeans/whatever are tucked in, and other times bell bottoms hide them. And yes, they do have a heel. They push me to just over medium height.

I'm tired of using words like 'cool' and 'freaky' and 'dude' and most of my customers have also outgrown them or never used them.

Otherwise, life's like running for a bus with one broken heel. I eat and drink by reaching out when I can, or I might not eat a bite and be on my feet more than 12 hours a day, including work in the kitchen. If I see or feel my waist or high-buttressed buttocks tending to plumpness I cut down. If it's sparse down there, I eat and drink more. A tight-tied apron when on the shop floor is a great comfort to my vanity.

The shop is revolutionary in how it's set up and what it sells, so is well known further away than Notting Hill Gate. Thus, as well as locals wanting to spend pounds in my deli, Saturdays also mean that many of the antique and vintage market's thousands of tourists and amateur collectors descend, wanting to take souvenir shots but spend little in the shop.

Those lox and bagels (sliced open at an angle, so the filling billows at you, perky and inviting) and hot salt-beef sandwiches are sold outside the shop as ploys for keeping them there.

Saturday's antique, vintage and junk stall-holders, inside the arcades and outside on the street, rely on my kitchen from very early. That's when most of their business is done, dealer to dealer. Tourists are keener on tat with Swinging London badges, even though that was the 60s, a decade ago. The cooler ones want a bargain with BIBA's defunct label or something second-hand by Mary Quant or by Carnaby Street's Lord John or I was Lord Kitchener's Valet. Clothes vintage and military sell to any bloke with long hair. Or bird with a crop.

Whoever or whatever they are, I hope they appreciate Portobello as more than a retail opportunity. It's entertaining, tatty, sometimes tacky, and needs a paint and scrub up but to me it's genuine London, untouched pre-war London.

Some of the costermonger families in the daily fruit and veg market that starts where the Saturday market ends at Elgin Crescent are 4th generation, descended from itinerant sellers of the ancient costard apple. The two open-fronted fish shops belong to the same family, and I see three generations with freezing, blue-cold hands gutting, boning and skinning, even when there's snow on the pavement.

As for the Saturday shenanigans, different women claim they were first to open an 'antique' shop or arcade, but it seems the area was long known as somewhere to buy the curious. That should be curios, because the story is that Notting Hill was where 18th and 19th century sailors came to sell those they had brought home.

Portobello Rd was once a track to a farm of that name.

This morning I know I'll be hammered on the deli floor about what happened during August's Carnival and the boy on the November bonfire and what I am doing to sort out these mysteries. Once I was dubbed the Deli Detective it stuck, and so do expectations I'll help solve local crimes.

All I know is that Freddy the Fire is the second teenager who's been found dead around here in the past months. And that whatever happened to them, both had been dead some time before their bodies were discovered.

As soon as I appear upstairs with the filled bagels, customers meld into one, vaulting from curiosity to accusations and rekindled suspicions. Before I answer, two more come in, a burly blonde bloke called Jeff and redheaded Helen.

Awkward to see them together.

I'd slept with both.

Had she blabbed? Had he? Did it matter in 1978?

It wasn't bed I thought about. Both had 'helped enquiries' in the past. One with social gossip, the other with unofficial police material. What might they want to tell me?

Would it be about Freddy?
Or might it be Richard Metcalfe?
His corpse almost put me out of business.

Chapter 2

●

Tuesday August 29th, 1978

The noise is dull but insistent, like the far-off splutter of an idling outboard motor. I open my eyes for the third time and again try to work out what it could be.

I know it's not a chiller or freezer in the delicatessen two floors below. It's something else, but what? Not knowing makes me edgy. After five years of living on Portobello Road I've learned always to be on guard. This nether part of Notting Hill Gate is never quite safe at night, certainly not after the Carnival parades of this past three-day weekend, when any one hot-blooded is still apt to be over excited. Outrageous and revealing costumes, steel drums, rum and ganja all contribute. Carnival's excesses have long been used as excuses for crimes of revenge and of corrosive class and race envy.

As the heavy Moroccan djellaba robe slips over my head I catch sight of the time. It's almost 2.45 am.

That makes it scarier.

I take two final silent steps into the pale light of the ground floor shop, lit from Portobello Road. There are no protective hoardings over the frontage. I'd agreed with locals that the social atmosphere had improved since the awful riots of the '76 Carnival and that boarding up could seem provocative.

It was a risk, but I got away with it. The internal

security system is working and would have warned of intruders long ago. I feel safer and punch in the deactivation code.

As I step down to the basement kitchen, my heart thumps. There's something sticky on the steps but I can't see what.

My breath stops when I see the thick fire door is ajar, jammed open by what I sense is a bottle. I pull at the door a little and the noise gets louder.

A machine is running yet because of Carnival we've been closed since Friday night. Why didn't I hear it before?

I free the door and turn on the kitchen lights.

I stifle a laugh, a common reaction to discovering a body.

The police should be told at once, I know. But my detecting instincts need feeding before anyone else sees what is before me. Notting Hill's police can't be trusted to get anything right or treat any incident as serious if it seems complicated.

Anyway, this is my kitchen. It's my body.

I'll take my time, although I know who it is at once.

The body of teenager Richard Metcalfe has been laid with care on the central preparation table in my kitchen, his bare arms across his chest. He's wearing a vivid red dress that's tight over his thighs and knee length, but there are slashes through it into his left chest, across his upper arm and up into his neck.

The sleeveless top has a deep neckline and a panel of fine pleats that swirls from the right shoulder past the waist and over the left hip where it curls into a rose. It's vintage and smart and reminds me how stars dress in old movies.

Much of the fabric is crumpled and damp as though it's been rinsed but not dried or ironed. Even though lined, which suggests something exclusive, it clings enough to show Richard wears nothing underneath it. Why has he been undressed and dressed again?

In spite of post-mortem lividity and some bruising, Richard is still blessed with skin the burnished gold of whipped wild honey. His leonine blonde hair is now streaked and matted with blood, much of it in blackened hanks, although it seems someone has tried to wash it. On one side there is a cruel gash like a crescent moon. It's gone through to the brain.

The polish on his nails is unchipped, so I don't think he's had to defend himself. His matching lipstick is unsmeared and when I look closer it's quite fresh.

His eyes are half open and even in death they shine like shooters, those biggest glass marbles of childhood. They combine a profound emerald green and the intense blue of rare Kashmir sapphires, each fenced with a double fringe of lacquer-black lashes.

When Richard lived his eyes were irresistible, even when you knew one direct look could be as fatal as the glance of a basilisk. You believed in angels if those blistering eyes favoured you. But it was the Devil you saw.

Richard was seraphic as a child but transfigured into a predator, tall, golden and addicted to the pursuit and capture of humans. His constant rehearsals of what he had to offer and how, where and to whom he wished to demonstrate its delights made him both feared and admired.

Not everyone appreciated his sexual predations, and Portobello's underground whisperers called him Golden Dick, but it was a jeer. Now it seemed one or more of his targets had chosen revenge. Which of the chased had turned? Who had made Portobello Road's gilded hunter into the hunted?

With no extraction fans working, the kitchen is warm and there's something of the headiness of an Indian spice and food shop. Remembrances of burned incense, perhaps? No. I recognise relics of what I've learned on Portobello is a chypre scent. The lingering base notes have the expected mossiness but isn't there a resonance of patchouli, that scent of youth and protest? Its intrusive and disturbing because, like the lipstick, it must have been applied while I was asleep upstairs. I keep my breath shallow to avoid any stink of decay that might also be present.

My eyes snap shut and my mind swirls as I fight to absorb the mysteries. My foot squelches in something on the floor. There are insane squirts of sauces from discarded plastic bottles. One of chocolate sauce had kept the door open, allowing the noise to escape and alert me two floors above. When I lift my head, I see the sauces have been used like ink. The tiled wall above the double sink is smeared with numbers and letters that look like a weird code. Explanations, warnings or the jabberings of insanity?

Then I spot what I should have seen at once. Across Richard's pelvis is my biggest Sabatier kitchen knife.

It's not placed as though for some ritual, but seems to have been dropped, abandoned in a hurry. Did I not notice it because knives are commonplace here?

And what about the sausage machine? There is prepared pork in the hopper and a length of casing is attached to the feeder tube but there's no clue to what was then planned.

Do the knife and the sausage machine have any relevance to why Richard Metcalfe is laid out on the table we use to make sandwiches and pizzas and cheesecakes?

Who has been here, and what has been interrupted?

Chapter 3

Saturday September 2, 1978

The deli was closed from last Tuesday morning until Friday while police investigated Richard's death. No-one believes it, but the mark-ups in a deli are some of the smallest on a High Street. A few more days and I might not have opened again.

With a backlog of August's Carnival crimes, and requirements for mountains of manual paperwork, the Notting Hill police want quick answers, easy solutions and certain convictions. You must be a multiple murderer or international child trafficker to get their full attention and even then there is a belief that the bigger you are the easier it is to get away with any crime. I reckon the police rely on Portobello's many communities preferring to sort out their own problems.

A dead 19-year-old in a dress in a deli kitchen is not the usual run of crimes but isn't enough to command the full weight of its detective force when there are no obvious clues as to who had murdered him, or why. No fingerprints, no bloody handprints, just a useless confusion of footprints that petered out on the steps from the kitchen, explaining the stickiness when I first went down. I reckon the police have given up but so far I have no sense I should be investigating instead, even though it was my kitchen that was so desecrated.

The one useful fact is that whoever laid out Richard in my kitchen had a key to my shop and knew the security codes. Oh, and that he had been dead for two if not three days by the time I found him.

Yet, he'd not been in my kitchen on Monday night before I checked the locks and went to bed. The locks and security codes have been changed now but this doesn't make me feel safer. Haven't you worried about the honesty of the blokes who work for locksmiths?

I don't sleep well.

The police tapes have gone and I am free to open the deli again. We needed Friday to clear up and check no fresh stock had passed its best.

On the last step down before opening the door to the shop floor I tighten my stomach and lips and hold my breath to prolong the expectation. Then I turn the lock and push.

As soon as the door swings enough to admit light, the smell hits. Ok, smell isn't quite the right word. Aroma might be better. Not fragrance though or scent. Both too fragile and girly. Smell is what everyone says: Oh, what a wonderful smell!

And this morning it's more wondrous than ever.

The long entrapment of the deli's smells has multiplied them into a mix as exotic and alluring as the most complicated eau de parfum.

Outside the walk-in Cheese Cabin in one corner there's seeping milk and mould promise from the crusts of huge, muslin-bandaged Cheddars, piercing pleasures from the smaller unbreeched blues. Through grilles on the side of the cabin come suggestions of the tramp's-foot stink of tawny, washed-rind cheeses that deliver surprising sweetness and satin to the tongue.

I open the cabin's door a little and mushroomy notes escape on the chilled air from wooden boxes of buttery Brie and Camembert, together with sharp warnings from those we'll have to sell today. I won't eat these two if they are ammoniacal but it's amazing how many believe that's the proper way, when Brie and Camembert are critical and runny rather than sweet and voluptuous. I tell staff never to argue.

I don't want to overwhelm the shop's other scented pleasures, so fasten the door, trying not to catch a whiff of our parade of small goats' milk cheeses, some in crumpled natural skins, some in charred ash or once-green herbs. Even a smidgen on my tongue tastes like licking a Billy goat's bottom in High Summer. It happens to others too, but not to most, because we sell heaps.

Now the exotica of a spice souk grab my throat. That's because we grind spices to order, cardamom, coriander or cumin seeds and cinnamon quills and such blends as the Middle East's clove-nail heightened baharat or Morocco's complicated ras el hanout, that sensual fusion of more than 20 of the most perfumed seeds, barks, petals, resins and stamens; traditionalists include hashish and the reputed aphrodisiac Spanish Fly. I avoid those two because they would cause more trouble than not amidst the social addicts of Portobello Road.

Modern versions often add chilli to baharat, which

means 'spice mixture' and to ras el hanout, which means 'top of the shop', the place where traders kept the most expensive spices. I don't follow this insidious craze because it's wrong, unknown where they come from.

Every morning we grind sweet spices and put them in pots about the shop. Those from last week must be replaced before we open.

I've been shamed as a renegade, a destroyer of traditional grocery provisioners. Perhaps it's because my deli is a culinary expression of the Permissive Society, but something I reckon morality campaigner Mary Whitehouse would approve. That's because the shop is open plan. It's thought a retailing revolution to have no counters or glass cabinets for staff to huddle behind and ignore you; my assistants and I mingle with the customers.

It's a 70s' food love-in, a kitchen Woodstock, but without Ravi Shankar and Arlo Guthrie. I'm faithful to Bill Haley, the Beatles, Little Richard and the late great Elvis, of course.

Open-faced chilled shelves offer customers direct access to salamis and sausages, pates, cooked meats, sauces, and fresh ingredients, almost none of which is pre-packed but are served or sliced to order.

Dry goods, the packets and bags and cans and bottles, are shelved above the chillers and on free-standing displays. Yep, there are few straight aisles, but I reckon that makes shopping more adventurous because you never know what's around the corner, inviting each customer to be an explorer. I love to help them find something. It's encouraging to hear 'What's new this week, Dan?'

We are pioneering ready meals. Chunky ratatouille, duck with cherry sauce and Coronation chicken, so far. My version of that classic adds canned mango, underpinning the mango chutney I include in the curry-mayonnaise. Using the same ingredient in different forms is something I do a lot, a reliable way to ensure both originality and flavour affinity.

Where you can see them, the walls are in wide diagonal stripes of black, white and purple. Thick-hewn planks on barrels support slicing machines, cash registers and special displays. Green and white enamel industrial lightshades hang from the black ceiling, and we play a mix of folk and rock'n'roll at very low volume. Can't afford to mishear a customer.

Most of the shop front concertinas out of the way when weather permits, making it harder to walk by its smells and sights.

It's a very good time to be selling specialty food. Inclusive holidays by jet to Spain or Italy have become more affordable over the past few years. Ingredients and dishes encountered in tavernas and salumerias, bodegas and trattorias are now expected on Notting Hill Gate's plates.

I'm happy to help.

Also, I take the trouble to pin shelf-labels with instructions for use, so uncertain customers can tutor themselves and not risk the ingredient shaming enjoyed by snobby staff in such as W H Cullen, By Appointment, where a young colonial seeking vegetables to roast on a Sunday, was told that 'pumpkin goes into beef, Sir. Not with it'.

I sell espresso coffees, made by Bella, a huge classic Elektra Belle Époque Q1, a tall golden metal dome topped with a high-winged eagle. There's no other in Portobello. It was expensive, very, but I judge its reflective gleams of polished brass and copper are enticing and welcoming.

Bella is well-lit and in front of a long pink mirror that multiplies the warmth of her charisma, and she's deep inside the shop, so customers for coffee wait surrounded by pastries and breads and everything else good to eat from the hand. I wonder why other delis don't sell espresso but recognise the coffee-bar fad of the 60s is well past.

Chapter 4

•

This Saturday morning my mind is more interested in Richard's murder and the frisson of knowing I am supposed to have no interest in solving it. I have time to ponder that. There is plenty of staff and two rather special overseers, Princess Luciana and Jeremy. Plus Trev at Bella's side, determined he is a barrister rather than a barista.

Luciana is a real princess, by marriage anyway. She's high-born Italian, a contessa in her own right, and was once married to a French prince. There are more than you might think. His family and such others as the Polignacs were given the rare privilege of all children being princes and princesses from birth. Same as the famiglia Pignatelli of Italy.

Luciana was amused when I combined her title and her birth and christened her La Principessa. This was soon shortened to LPP and then the lavatorial humour of the young colonials I prefer to employ to ensure willing customer service changed that to 'La pee-pee' and then to 'Wee-wees'. Hard to credit the amount of laughter this causes amongst them, and this is what they call her when they think neither she nor I can hear.

Luciana is tall, majestic without effort, blonded by the bottle, assisted by discreet Brazilian pioneers of the scalpel, and imbued with a sense of superiority that is implacable. She's been some man's princess from birth.

Her passage down Portobello Road's hill from her palazzino in Chepstow Villas is a procession of one. Her eyes focus on nothing and no-one, yet crowds part and watch as she moves through them. She is fond of wearing something flowing or fluttery, a swirling cape or a swagger-back coat from the 50s. A lot of floaty silk in summer.

Princess Luciana arrives at the deli around 10.00 and takes a ristretto coffee, very short and almost caffeine-free when made the correct way, and sweet with natural sugars if it's decent coffee, as are our Colombian Arabica beans. These are never more than medium roasted. Anything darker and you taste the burn not the bean.

La Principessa sits on a high stool against the shelf on a wall of the cheese cabin and drinks her ristretto the correct Italian way, in two sips and without putting the cup into the saucer between them. She sometimes takes a cappuccino before midday and shakes her head at anyone who orders one after that time. She expects the most louche local to have breakfasted by then and so order something without milk.

After taking her cappuccino, or instead of it, she commands a bottle of Chianti Superiore, which she tipples with determined constancy but discretion, her glass always seeming half full.

At about two, she might take a slice of aged Parmesan or half a buffalo-milk mozzarella with a few olives, some carrot sticks, a crusty roll and a saucer of single-estate Tuscan olive oil from the groves of her patrician friends the Marchese and Marchesa de' Frescobaldi, whose Chianti castelli are where Queen Victoria and now Prince Charles and other royals have escaped to paint in private.

'I never paint with them,' Luciana says. 'I watch, and by watching I learn what I do not like about watercolours. Mainly the colours . . . and then there's the water . . .'

At her stool she trades in the highest quality gemstones and jewellery, using the wiles, nods and few words only initiates understand. Jewellers' loupes are forever at their eyes, but I never see money in their hands.

I allow her to use the deli because Luciana sees and hears everything. Her sharpened social sensibilities were honed in the brittle salons, private yachts and luscious dining rooms of haute-Europe, as much for self-protection as for salacious interest, she claims. Her business associates and smart friends are good customers, too.

Tall, fair-haired Jeremy is South African, about 30, and wears abbreviated sleeves, knee-length safari shorts and long socks regardless of season. He manages the staff and is adept at sensing a slight movement from Luciana that indicates she has spotted a shoplifter or a bill avoider or a loser who's chosen to smoke dope in the shop. Nick-named the Blonde Beast by those working for him, Jeremy learned his skills both in the South African army and tracking game over veldts.

In W11 the combined wiles of a hunter and a graduate of Europe's aristo-ciety are invincible. Neither cares about being known as a snitch. I lose little to theft while these two are riding the range.

Trev came to me after last year's Carnival. On the Tuesday morning afterwards, the council's workers were still cleansing Portobello Road and I was sloshing the pavement outside the deli with a mop.

A thin but confident voice told me I was doing it wrong. My critic was short and stocky, without being fat. I think slab not slob because he had no discernible waist, chest or buttocks. He had his baker's boy cap well down, and reeked of fabric conditioner used to excess, a certain sign he was from the Council estates up Portobello either side of Westbourne Grove. I wasn't happy about being cheeked by what looked like a 12-year-old.

'Reckon you can do it better, mate?'

'Anyone could, mate. You gotta get those chairs on the tables, innit?'

I held out the mop, impatient with the interruption.

'Better show me how, mate!'

I left him to it. Not my job I told myself, but it was hard to get anyone else to pick up a mop and bucket.

He did a very good job, the tables with equal spaces between them, the chairs aligned and the bottom stretch of their legs washed and shined. He's a natural neatnik. The street front is as spotless as a Portobello Road pavement can be, so is still smeared, scratched, pitted and patched, but you can tell where the deli begins and ends.

I'm so surprised and pleased I hear myself telling

him he's got a job, part-time but permanent if he wants.

'Good one, mate!' he says.

I bait him. 'Funny how that word mate is used to mean everything from fuck off to I love you.'

He's outraged. 'You reckon I'm saying I love ya?'

'Mate!!!!'

He gets it and snuffles his amusement. I see his eyes have the colour and transparency of Baltic amber and shine with humour. Nice, but what else? I sensed loneliness, a pleading to be liked. Or was it my over-empathy over working? I ask if he's had any breakfast. He shrugs but his eyes flicker towards the croissants, pastries and cakes.

'C'mon then, croissants and a cappuccino?'

'Yeah, alright,' he says, as though it's what he would have ordered anyway. I'm certain he's never tasted either. But he's curious and adventurous and this is number one in my book. Well, number one and number two I suppose.

I watch his reflection in the mirror behind the espresso machine as I froth the milk, skimmed milk because it's protein not fat that makes the best foam. He looks like the proverbial awe-struck kid in a toy shop and moves to stand closer, perhaps for comfort.

'Ain't never bin in a place like this.'

'Why not?'

'Too posh.'

'Says who?'

'You just know. Around here.'

'Everybody eats, posh or not,' I say, carrying his coffee to an outside table.

I hadn't asked about chocolate or cinnamon on top. Rather than embarrassing him I've sprinkled on chocolate and put down two warm croissants in a basket with pats of butter and a pot of shop-made strawberry jam on a plate.

'I'm Dan by the way,' I say, wanting to calm his panic at what faces him.

'Trev,' the boy says. Of course he does.

I see his eyes cloud. 'It's ok to dunk,' I say. He sniggers, snuffling his pointy nose rather rodent like, and shuffles himself to greater comfort.

'You know, mate, that expresso thing needs polishing.'

'It's espresso.'

'It still needs a touch up, innit? Thought the deli-detective would have spotted that. Mate.'

Chapter 5

Wednesday September 6th, 1978

It's chaos. Well, Wednesday is always chaos because so many suppliers deliver. I couldn't do without them, yet they are a burden on top of all else. After being closed last week, my stock levels are a mess, short of fresh produce we couldn't buy then, which also means the kitchen is still catching up.

I do the job most deli owners don't have time to do. I meet, I greet. I keep a moving eye so there is never a customer who leaves because they can wait no longer to be served, never shelves that are untidy or bread shelves empty while there's stock in the storeroom. I'm the spare hand who leaps in to tidy the cheeses after a rush, rehangs the salamis, picks up the spilled basket. And sweep and wash because everyone else is 'a bit busy'. That leaves manager Jeremy and his staff to take money without distractions.

I also check everything that comes into the deli because short weight and overcharging is rife. At least we ask a customer if they will accept a 'little over' or a 'little under' but we are at the mercy of any supplier who is a bit fly, who knows and uses tricks hardened criminals wouldn't recognise. It's not the grafting artisans and specialist companies who supply us but the blokes they get to sell on their behalf. I could tell you stories all day. But not this morning.

It's a few minutes after nine. I am in a white van that has driven overnight from Rungis market in Paris stuffed with French cheeses. It's a couple of young blokes, one public school, the other less so, who saw London was ready for something more than block Cheddar and Danish blue. They bring me bleu d'Auvergne and Pont l'Eveque, Gaperons (with and without beards) triple-crème St Andre and ghastly goat cheeses – no wonder some are called crottins. They look like the 'droppings' after which they are named.

Customers love these regular revelations of French cheese, and some come in just to ask what has arrived from Paris. I couldn't buy from them last week, so they expect a good order this one. If they can't rely on me, they'll desert me for another retailer.

As I start smelling and tasting there's a long moan from the shop, interrupted by loud pleas for attention.

'He's gone. I've lost him. And the bastards won't help.'

I tell the White Van Boys to pack up a selection and give the invoice to Jeremy to pay in cash. That'll have to be checked, even though I'd like to trust them.

The moaner is Lena, who's in most days to shop for the grand houses in which she cleans and polishes. She's a plump bottle-blonde but does little else to her hair. It's worn too long and too thin and hangs unkempt in knotted serpents, emphasising a fury of broken veins on her nose and cheeks. She always smells of furniture polish.

Lena's agitated and I put an arm around her. I ask

her to tell me what's wrong, steering her to the back of the shop.

'Freddy. It's Freddy, my boy. He ain't come home.'

'Since when?'

'Monday, Carnival day. Went out, didn't come back and the police . . .'

'They made you wait . . .'

'Yeah, so I can be sure. Wait three days they said, but it's 10 now and he still ain't come home. He's only 17, but they say there's nothing they can do because there ain't no clues. Lazy bastards.'

Constant collision with private lives is what's so special about a food shop, a good food shop. It soon becomes a confessional and counselling service at the centre of a borderless village. Some revel in it, others flee and make me wonder what their secrets might be. This seems more serious. Richard is discovered and now Freddy is missing. There's a mystery about two teenage boys and both cases are associated with Carnival.

I've already been warned against doing any investigation into Richard's murder back in August. Detective Inspector John Harding from Notting Hill police in Ladbroke Grove has told me that twice. Yet, I'm feeling like my secret hero Batman, signalled into action and now poised in pursuit, caped, masked and teetering at the top of a piste, a steep, dangerous black one. Without Bruce Wayne's butler Pennyworth to caution me and no Robin to slap if something goes wrong.

In the past I've helped the police by passing on

something I've overheard in the deli or extracted by careful questioning of a customer. I reckon Harding wants to establish what I know that he does not, not least because it'll make his job easier.

My answer is that I'm keeping out of it. So far.

None of the Portobello networks is helping, not the antique and junk dealers, not the costermongers, not the cannabis dealers, not even the career-criminal families that make certain they're part of all the other groups.

This could be because Portobello Road's community spirit means whatever is most convenient to the comfort of most, whatever the cost to morality, to good sense or to an ill-placed individual.

However, there are mysteries to be solved. I feel a tell-tale tingle climbing over my shoulders and up my throat. I reckon Bruce Wayne felt this when he saw the Bat Signal. Except, in Freddy's case there's nothing for me to solve until he is found.

It's hard to convince Lena I'm not the person she should be talking to, and I must send her home with little hope.

Chapter 6

Luciana and I are expected at Richard's memorial service. As we leave, Trev insists on joining us.

'Them others can work Bella now.'

'Clever Trevor,' I mock, emphasising the rhyme. 'You've done that so you can slink away.'

Blanking me and my witty quip, he says, 'We'll discover something.'

'Oh no we won't. We're not there to play detectives.'

The way Luciana and Trev smirk at one another suggests I am wrong.

Richard Metcalfe's parents greet us at the door of the hall they've hired. It's deep in North Kensington and as grey and pointless as the ceremony is likely to be. There are rumours of the kiss of peace and of having to profess love to those sitting about you.

'Grisly,' Luciana declares.

The dead youth's father is broken. Johnny Metcalfe's short body has swollen into a tub of putty, his face falling in a collier de chien that conceals the knot of his tie. He has swapped his usual blue blazer and flannel trousers for a pin-stripe suit that advertises its familiarity with mothballs.

Luciana's handshake does more for him than whatever others are murmuring. He worked in India and believes in the old systems, in titles and orders of precedence, but also in the mutual respect of all classes for each other.

Johnny turns teary blue eyes up to acknowledge

Luciana and drops and lifts his head, as though she were royalty.

His wife Belinda warns everyone not to hug him. She means her, too, and leans back when physical contact threatens.

Belinda is known as The Scream, even by those with no knowledge of Norwegian art. Her face is lantern jawed, tight skinned, what Luciana compares to il maschera de Mussolini, but her squareness is not the real shock. Beneath a chevron of cheekbones like unbaked sausage rolls, her mouth is that of an infant. It opens only upwards in a perpetual tiny 'O' of silenced screaming.

Today it's daubed bright red, which heightens the pain of bereavement apparent on her eyelids.

Luciana is bossy and restricts us to the back row and sits upright, her regal posture giving a panoramic view. We nod and make appropriate gestures of sorrow to whomever turns to scrutinise us. Sometimes the attention is because my ankle-length, black-leather coat squeaks when I move.

Trev said it makes me look like a dick. Of the detective type, I hope.

I recognise several generations of costermongers from the market's stalls. There's a group of junk and vintage dealers in bright colours and flashy costume jewellery (Fabulous, dahling, sold one rather better than that last week!). Meredith and her son Jem sit beside the Metcalfes, and his Ivy-League togs are very different from others of his age. Meredith's self-interest is manifested by her pointing out to Johnny how allergic she is to mothballs.

The younger attendees are self-conscious, fashionable and long-haired. Tie-dyed bell bottom trousers or super-short minis with crocheted tops are abundant, and gender assignment is a challenge. Pools of kohl and mascara help defeat categorisation. Patchouli's penetrating presence could come from any of them.

Richard is also present, a grey powder in a small glass mixing bowl spot lit in front of its erstwhile nest, a neo-classical tea caddy in rosewood with ivory fittings.

'Take special note of whom seems too sad and quiet,' Luciana commands. 'Trev, you do that. Dan, make a note of everyone who is the most distressed – you know, crying, weeping, expecting his or her back to be rubbed and patted, whatever that's supposed to achieve.'

'What'll you do?' Trev asks.

'Both,' she says, not minding his cheeky challenge.

I absorb little of the service except to learn that today would have been Richard Metcalfe's 20th birthday and that the hall had been hired for a party. More is said about his presumed spirit life than about his existence in this world.

'Not much help to us,' declares Luciana as we stand to one side to watch the exodus. Some hurry away, others stay and gossip.

'Help us with what?' I wonder.

'Finding his killer,' Trev shouts, as though to a

stupid child. 'We are private dicks finding who killed a public dick.'

'Good line,' smiles Luciana.

'Great,' I say. 'That's what everyone's going to think now, even if it's not true.'

Batman's skis have started downhill without me.

Or is it the other way around?

On the southern side of the Westway viaduct, Royal Kensington rather than North Kensington I like to think, I am angry and silent as we walk along avenues of mansions that bonus-swollen bankers are returning to private palaces after long nightmares as grotty bed-sits. Then in just a few steps we are overwhelmed by the racket of Ladbroke Grove. A single puddle of low autumn sunlight does little to soften the shock.

'Have the police interviewed everyone who had a key to the deli?' asks Luciana.

'Or everyone who knows someone with a key . . . no, I don't think they did.'

That's never been something I worried about. I've always given keys to staff because I do not want to open the doors at 6.30 every morning. Anyway, isn't trusting people with keys supposed to make them more loyal?'

'So naïve,' Luciana mutters. She pulls her sleeveless mink cape about her, as though barricading herself from my idiocy.

'Anyway, I'm starting to think there might have been more than one of them,' I say. 'You know how heavy a dead body is. '

'A 'body' is usually dead, I think you'll find.'

Trev breaks us up. 'What about them two girls in the next row?'

I have no idea where he's going with that and start to say so when he makes a little leap of triumph and shakes a spread-fingered hand as though ridding it of water.

'That's it, innit? I thought they was crying but most of the time they was trying to stop laughing.' He's about to add another 'innit' but I stop that. 'What was the joke?'

'One of them thinks she's well got away with something, like well got away . . .' He turns to Luciana for the acknowledgement he's not getting from me.

'Exactly what I think,' she agrees.

Not wanting to seem I hadn't been working, I ask if they noticed the man dressed only in black, who stood apart with his head bowed, shaking it from side to side.

'So ostentatious, all black,' says Luciana.

'Yeah, I seen 'im,' Trev says. He crinkles his eyes and shakes a finger as he remembers. 'And . . . yeah and, then when he caught the eye of a couple of them older boys, he cringed but they smiled something wicked . . . like someone was licking their balls. Ooops, sorry princess!'

The real-world cracks into our thoughts. Overhead, two Underground trains pass on the bridge across Ladbroke Grove, shrieking metal and thumping suspensions amplified in the maw between the rails and street. It's disorientating and then fumes from red double-decker buses envelope us. They mix with the pall of old frying oil and haze from the takeaways.

I feel dirty and exposed. I want to be alone to think. I also need to be polite and am about to invite them back for tea and cakes when Luciana stands back, shrugs her coal-black cape about her shoulders and changes the subject.

'Two things, Daniel. Your young man here needs better clothes. An apron and a cap don't hide his poverty of style. And he must be exposed to beauty. Men are always obsessive about neatness and hygiene when they have no understanding of beauty.'

She ignores Trev's protest.

'Look at his hands, Dan. Show me another teenage boy in W11 or W10 with cuticle-free nails.'

Luciana turns to block the sun from Trev. He can't avoid her. 'You iron your handkerchief and the laces of those things you wear on your feet. I expect you iron your underpants, too, and your socks. Non e vero?'

Trev pleads without words. I see everything is true.

'Mate,' I say, 'this isn't criticism, it doesn't mean...'

He disappears under his cap. There's reluctant amusement dancing in those eyes. 'So, does it mean I'll be good enough to be your henchman, does it, mate? Three of us solving crimes together, innit?'

Luciana strikes without mercy. 'Your 'innit' will have to go. It's meaningless. And henchmen do crimes, not solve them.'

Trev pops his head out. 'I knew that!'

She tightens her lips. If she'd been one of the local gang-bitches she would have mumbled, 'Yeah, right!'

She tells him that before he's either henchman or accomplice he needs to look and smell better. 'I've watched you for a year and you still look like a benefit scrounger. You can't solve crimes looking like that,' she says. 'And that after-shave is foul, whatever some old boxer says.'

I try to interrupt but Luciana is on a mission. 'I'll take him to Marks and Spencer on High Street Kensington and into Kensington Market . . . it's not all old kaftans and hand-woven shoulder bags. Some of the stalls have high-end bargains. West End names, Roma and Milano.' She pauses to wrinkle her nose. 'Even New York.'

'Places I ain't never been to, boss.'

Playing La Principessa stupenda, Luciana swings her pendant watch across Trev's face. It's spangled with baguettes of emerald and sapphire and is suspended on a sautoir of peacock-hued black Tahitian pearls. 'Exposure to beauty? It'll be the making of him. A haircut, too, don't you think? Come along, umm…Trev.'

Trev turns to me. 'You see, mate? Mrs Princess sees what you didn't. I didn't want to wash your bleeding street, y'know. I wanted to be a detective, like you.'

Luciana takes Trev's willing arm and strides him towards the 52-bus stop while instructing him in the advantages of stranded mink over full-pelt mink, her hand guiding his as she demonstrates the richer, glossier texture of her stranded fur.

He seems interested. Who knew?

Suddenly there's a hand on my shoulder and it's not trying to make friends.

Chapter 7

'You seem very interested in everyone and everything,' a voice says, its tone as frosted as the wind.

'And you are?' I ask, straightening my shoulders.

It's the Man in Black. Tall, tanned and fit. His well-fleshed hands suggest physical strength and my stomach quivers until I see his blue eyes deflated by my pathetic counter-challenge. They flitter with anxiety as he continues a threat that sounds rehearsed. 'Never mind my name. I know you, mate. You push y'nose in, innit? Right where it's not wanted, eh?'

He waves a straight but trembling finger across my face.

'Here's some interesting facts for you, Sherlock,' he says, his index finger working like a windscreen wiper. 'There's lots of people around the Portobello what would rather forget Richard Metcalfe.'

'But someone murdered him. Don't you think...?'

'Them same folk thinks it's a bloody good thing he's dead. And they also thinks it would be a bloody great shame if you don't back off. No-one wants to know who dunnit. See? Or cares.'

He glances over his shoulder, then flips off my stitched leather hat. 'That might help you see things better.'

I reach to stop it rolling onto the road and see a surly knot of onlookers across the street. Most have hurried from the memorial service to takeaways, seeking mourning-after comforts, and are now sucking at fatty lips and fingers.

The Man in Black taps his finger to a nostril and looks across at the huddlers, who shuffle forward attempting to look staunch. Are these the ones who overheard Trev saying we are detectives?

Thinking this remote support makes his message clear, the Man in Black dodges traffic to the other side of the Grove and disappears. The pavement is soon clear of his posse, too.

The thing is, although I'd like to solve Richard's murder, I've not said or done much about it so far. So why would anyone need to warn me off? The situation doesn't seem real, but then reality never did have much foothold in Portobello's tittle-tattle, innuendo and lies.

I'm trying to unravel the meaning of the warning when a car slows down. The track-suited driver honks and wiggles his clenched fist in the international sign suggesting the only sex I can lay my hand on is my own. There's just time to see the car is stacked with old sporting equipment. I know who he is.

Barry was once a Sports Master at St Benedict's, the school where many of the young mourners went to or had gone to earlier. Now he deals in vintage and antique sporting goods and clothes from one of Portobello's arcades.

Didn't recognise him out of the clammy t-shirt and bunched up shorts he wears when he jigs and jogs about in the deli. I expect it's the last I'll see of him in there.

Why is he also threatening me?

. . .

There's a good rule I use for murder investigations. It's this, that the fastest way to uncover a murderer is to find out everything about the victim. Not world-shattering or original but that's why it works.

My personal take is that solving crimes is the same as inventing a new dish. First, I assemble the ingredients, the equivalent of a detailed understanding of the crime and who might be involved. Then I identify the method that puts them together in the right way, taking time to get the balance right, like peeling, toasting, marinating in a kitchen, any technique to get each one understood and identifiable.

Third, I serve up the result to the right patrons, trusting the ingredients and method work together to give pleasure, in this case meaning my pleasure in exposing the bad boys or girls.

The two street challenges move me closer to when I stop thinking and start doing what the police are not. Perhaps I will ferret out Richard Metcalfe's secrets. I'll find what a 19-year-old boy did to become known as Golden Dick, and why some want to forget.

If the rule is right, all this should help me identify who did what, whodunnit as the paperbacks say. I feel the tingle over my shoulders again.

I'm also being practical. The sooner this is solved, the sooner I'll feel safe again. It's not just the murderer who might be a threat. Richard's friends and foes both seem vindictive. That's double jeopardy – and more.

Just what are they keeping to themselves? However

bad Richard was, surely it's over now he's dead?

Deep-frying, exhaust fumes and a disgusting gust of wet soap powder and conditioner from a laundrette catch in my throat. A hacking cough starts, reminding me how life changes in a blink on these streets. Then I see a group of youths and their pelmet-thighed girls is eyeing me. They are moving to isolate me, the way a pack of hyenas does to take out the weakest animal. I feel as though I've crossed a border, entered a foreign country without the safety of a passport.

It's not far to walk back to the shop, but I step out into the traffic and shake my hat to hail a taxi.

Chapter 8

The deli works its comforting magic the moment I'm through the door. Even the efficiency of the extractor from the basement kitchen can't vent away all the aroma (right word this time) of our fresh-baked pizza, not floppy pizza but authentic thick crusted pizza made by Maria, our Neapolitan treasure. The rich tomato pulp topping and the black-peppery Tuscan olive oil she ladles into, under and over the yeast-bloomed dough are celebrations of all she was denied as a poor child, when her mother could make bread, but her father could put little on it.

We cut individual squares of Maria's peasant pizzas as big as a hand and as thick as a hen's egg, direct from roasting trays. One of these gratifies W11's urban peasants in ways thin-crust pizza never could. The tops are sumptuous, sodden with that tomato and olive oil, chewy with splodges of tender, true mozzarella. There are hidden salt-mines of anchovy fillets, drifts of correct dried oregano, pockets of rolled ham or salami, black olives and authentic Grana Padano, the lesser cousin of Parmigiano. I like this cubed rather than grated on my pizza, so these explode on my tongue.

I've found it best not to share with customers that I prefer Grana Padano to Parmigiano because it smells less like vomit. You've never thought that? Smell them close up…

I claim culinary droit de Seigneur and lever out a first, double-crusted corner piece and disappear upstairs to my flat while the pizza is still hot enough to have to toss between my fingers. With a glass of rugged red from anywhere in the world, nothing else is needed, not one of poet Omar Khayyam's boughs, not even a 'thou'.

In minutes I'm in my first-floor sitting room, sprawling in my body-hugging beanbag, a riot of purple and green Marimekko blooms against a rampage of psychedelic posters aswirl with the rest of the spectrum. I play Tina Turner loud, celebrating her escape from the enslavement of Ike.

I'm enjoying the uncouthness of chewing with open lips and slurping the wine, when I spy the tip of a big, padded envelope. It's been tucked between the cushions of ancient tapestry, kilim scraps and mirrored Indian embroidery that hope to give comfort to my Edwardian chesterfield.

The envelope is something I shouldn't have. I owe another favour to my friend Jeff, one of Notting Hill Gate's junior detectives. He might be the only public-spirited policemen there, and views illicit sharing of police records as a worthwhile balance to the incompetence he sees daily. Others do worse favours, he says.

I abandon the pizza and wine, twisting to my side so I can release myself from the embraces of the beans with some decorum, and rush to the kitchen to clean my hands. The rough swipe of a blue-chequered tea towel does my face, too.

When I tear open the envelope, police crime-photos of Richard's corpse slither and flip-flop out. I hadn't asked for them, but Jeff knows I like case details, however much I promise not to interfere. My Bat Flight down the ski slope has passed the point of no return. Tina is too much, and I shut her off.

It's shocking to see Richard again. I pour more wine and swig as I walk around the images, snatching quick glances. Why so abject? What's frightening me?

I change my fear to determination. If I'm not prepared to look at things like this, I shouldn't have opened the envelope. And if I'm not prepared to look at these images, I'm doing nothing about the duet of post-memorial threats.

It's not just me at risk. The shop is endangered, too, and everyone who works in it. It's easier for a determined enemy to target the shop and its workers rather than to hurt me. Perhaps it's done with less conscience because it is indirect. That might seem unfair but life's unfair.

Look at what's happened to me.

I'm not saying it was unjust that I had prostate cancer so young, at 36. It's neither just nor unjust that I'm alive when I could be dead or dying in horrid discomfort. What is unjust and unfair is how doctors fooled me into the treatment they wanted, rather than what I could have chosen.

Oh, they got rid of the cancer. But the price was too high. They didn't tell the truth about the feminising and demeaning side effects of testosterone suppression, the 'therapy' that cuts off the male hormone that's believed to feed prostate tumours. I wasn't given the opportunity to avoid it.

At the end of one of many weeks of helplessness, when all I'd been able to eat was what I tore off a loaf of wholemeal bread, moulding by the end of that week, I longed more than ever for the certainty and simplicity of the comic books that were so important before television.

Batman and Superman, Superboy and Captain Marvel and Captain Kidd, The Phantom . . . Their stories in bold pictures and few words made sense because good always won and that's what I needed to believe if I was to survive.

But I couldn't fly, wasn't a millionaire in a mansion with a cave under it, had no magic word of empowerment like SHAZAM!

Instead, I was depressed, frightened and tearful – a few more of the unacknowledged horrors that low or zero testosterone can bring.

Grumpy old men aren't doing it on purpose but can be unrecognised victims of natural hormone depletion. That can be reversed if a doctor cares to do so. Few do.

My comic-book memories dredge up two Golden Rules once stamped on the back of my hand at Sunday School. One said Deeds not Words. The other was longer and so the writing was smaller and got smudged, but I learned that too.

Do Unto Others As Ye Would That They Should Do Unto You. Is that right? Never mind. You know the one.

As a goal, as a reason to survive, I hooked on to those sayings and decided to live my life by those words.

There's no question of being a round-the-clock Dark Avenger. I just hope to put things right when I can, and get the bad people identified. My new quest is to find out who killed Richard Metcalfe, because it looks as though no-one else will.

I mean, think about Richard's parents, about Johnny and Belinda Metcalfe, and the bewildered sadness they endure every waking moment. It chills me to imagine how they feel, when everyone on Portobello Road knows the reputation their son had and how his body had been abandoned in my kitchen.

Vaulting empathy is a consequence of my struggle with testosterone suppression. A savvy endocrinologist prescribed replacement testosterone and that saved my mind and my life, but enhanced empathy remains. I weep more than other men because I understand more than I want about another's distress.

Sometimes my sympathies are for perpetrators and murderers and what brought them to their crimes.

Such opinions are not always popular.

Chapter 9

Even in the prints the Metcalfe boy is special. In life every muscle was as solid as alabaster yet seemed to billow with the luminosity of moonstone, the sort of skin Ingres loved to paint. He also had charm, charisma, humour, a killer smile and impeccable manners. The full arsenal.

I've had years to know Richard and perhaps working through this will help discover what's happened.

His parents were customers of the deli and when he was 15 he asked me for an evening and weekend job.

I watched him mesmerise customers for weeks before I recognised he was as heartless and keen-eyed as a kestrel, a golden-haired raptor, whose objectives were only the pleasures of the hunt and the kill.

When I saw him leave with goodies he had, well, stolen is the word for it, I ignored it. Just as I did when I saw him short-changing customers and then pocketing the difference because the people he stole from also knew it and ignored it. They were paying for the pleasure of having his attention.

Luciana and Jeremy weren't here then, and the assistants of the time worshipped him because they knew they'd never once have the courage to do what he did daily.

Sometimes he was content just to tease and then watch a man or woman blush or fluster and say something silly. Other times flattery and innuendo saw customers spending twice what they intended.

He didn't care if he was the victor.

I was a dupe because I realised that many people chose to shop in Dan's Deli because he was there. I made more than I lost through his predations and so ignored them. Until the day he targeted me.

Already as tall as me, he pinned me to the wall by pushing his thigh against mine. I was standing by the safe in the basement while I counted out the cash float there. I always cashed up around 6pm, so there was little money in the tills while we were open at night.

I was shocked and then embarrassed, because my heart beat faster and I held my breath. I was no longer a milky-breathed teenager grateful for sexual release with anything warm or that stood still. Yet, he exuded a physicality that overwhelmed me and persuaded me also to forget he was underage.

In a flash my mind unleashed memories of the repressed pleasures of sweaty longings in teenage rugby scrums, which encourage but pretend to forbid sexualised male contact. It was the tension of long, late aimless talks with schoolboy friends when every chance to give and get pleasure was subjugated to what others might think if they knew what we wanted. Many guys will recognise this but won't admit it to their wives.

I couldn't bear the power of Richard's eyes and turned away. He lifted his head and stretched his lips into his killer smile and then threaded fingers through my hair. He was too old to be a pretty child pleading for a treat, but this seemed his intent. He flicked back his hair, so it hung behind each shoulder and then hooded those piercing eyes to stare down at me, magnetic but malevolent.

He didn't smell of a teenage boy's boiling crotch or rotting feet or sebaceous skin and hair. He was fresh, sweet, like a grassy midsummer meadow and this made everything else seem natural. I closed my eyes to breathe him in and leaned forward to meet his lips. . . And then something intervened.

Hot anger shot into my throat. I wanted to lash and slash him to extinction, but a flash of insight told me my fury was not at Richard but at the sexual uncertainties I had been sentenced to by my testosterone depletion. Even if I wanted him, I wasn't sure I could. Thus, a welcome sense of dignity also played some part.

I didn't dare reject Richard outright or with any of the anger I felt. There was too much risk of payback if his feelings were hurt. I gave him a reason that saved his face. I joked that if I did it with him, I'd have to do it with everyone in the shop.

As further assurance, I added that he should try again, when he wasn't working for me. We both laughed and he promised he would. That hadn't happened.

With hindsight I see that his prey, yes, including me, were victims of the Portobello Syndrome, the intoxicating cupidity that you alone will own something rare and beautiful.

It's a hunger to be initiated into a closed circle of admirers of a Chiparus bronze of a dancer, to be one of the privileged few to own a sumptuous jewel fashioned by Rene Lalique before he pressed glass, to use silver from George IV's extravagant Regency, to own an ancient book or understand the intricacies of Forbidden Stitching on a Qing Emperor's silken Dragon Robe.

When you find and own such treasure, you can be the king or maharajah, the actress or courtesan, the explorer, politician, playboy or sportsman who treasured it before you. There seems to be no shame in committing whatever fraud, theft or other sin it takes to drown in your dreams.

Richard Metcalfe was such a prize. He was willing to be discovered and adored, quite as much as any of the thousands of objects of lust in Portobello's large and small stalls.

Did he also suffer from Portobello Syndrome?

What did Richard covet?

Or was he interested only in being bait for helpless hunters of his beauty?

Chapter 10

Killing Richard Metcalfe isn't mere murder, it's a sin against Creation, as awful as slashing an Old Master or stamping on natural pearls. He was an evil sod, but such beauty shouldn't be so defiled.

I refill my tumbler and then shuffle the pictures. When I see close ups of the dead boy it's sometimes a struggle to keep down the wine and pizza. At least there are none of the autopsy or afterwards.

I say it out loud. 'How could anyone?'

I don't know how long I've been overwhelmed by the clash of beauty and violence in the images when Luciana and Trev burst in, pink and loud with their new friendship and tales of shopping.

Luciana sees what's on the table and floor and turns away, waving her hands across her face like manic fans. After deep breaths she's composed and walking around the images as calm as if assessing a Renaissance palazzo's restored knot garden.

Trev is distressed and fussy. He sorts the prints into a more intelligent order than mine. He's not examining them, just shooting quick, troubled looks as he arranges them by subject, close-up, medium and long shot. It's obvious that more than the disorder that disturbs him.

Luciana has dressed him in blues, a knitted navy-blue top with a horse-and-rider logo worn over a lighter blue, button-down, Oxford-cloth shirt, stiff indigo jeans and leather-soled sneakers in

Cordovan red-brown with a fringe and tassels. Rockports, I expect.

The cap has gone and I see his hair is dark chestnut, which emphasises his amber eyes. What I thought was pasty skin instead is a clear ivory, delicate rather than unwholesome. Trust Luciana to get it right, although to be fair navy-blue is flattering to any man.

He's standing straighter too, but he's jittery and sweaty.

'Get over it,' I say.

'I will, mate' he answers.

What is it about the corpse of a teenage boy in a dress that's unsettling him? Is it getting him turned on? Richard's head is bashed in, his neck and chest are slashed and much of his body is discoloured. Still, this is Portobello Road, so you never quite know.

Luciana has pulled off her mink cape and thrown it onto the dining table. The fur's slick weight drags it to the floor. She toes it under the table and then chooses close-ups of the injuries and puts them on the table. I ask if she'd like more light but she signals me to be quiet.

Trev tutts, picks up Luciana's fur, folds it onto a chair and then pins the images of the lettering from the deli's kitchen onto a cork noticeboard at the top of my stairwell. When I ask what he's looking for, he stumbles to ask how I got the images.

'You've got a lot to learn,' I say, and he resists when I try to pull the prints from the board. He snatches them back.

'Learn what?'

'Around here no-one asks where anything comes from . . . not on Portobello Road, they don't.'

Luciana interferes on a different tangent. 'How long have you lived around here, Trev?' I note she has less trouble with his name.

''Ages. On and off. Why?' He's mumbling over his shoulder, not happy to have his thoughts interrupted.

'Just wondering how well you knew this young man,' Luciana continues.

'Seen him around. Couldn't miss him.'

I repeat Luciana's question. 'How long have you lived around here?'

'Most of me life. In me Dad's gaff. Them council flats, them brick ones, just up the Portobello. Right now he's banged up for thieving. I live there so we can keep the place.' I sense there's some relief in his voice that the subject has changed.

'We?'

'Me and me Mum sometimes. She's over 'ammersmith way. Mum split and took me when I was about four or five. The old man's a bit of a bastard with his fists when he's pissed. I liked coming back to see him because of the stuff in the market stalls and arcades. Didn't know what it was, but.'

'So instead of finding out, you iron your underpants.'

Trev shrugs off Luciana's scorn. 'I wanted to know, because it's like playing detective, innit? That's what I really wanted but it takes time to read them detective books and they miss out stuff on the telly. The cops wouldn't hire a runt like me, but being a detective still seemed like a right good game.'

'This isn't a game, tesoro,' says Luciana.

'If you say so,' he says.

Luciana persists. 'Anyway, you didn't answer. How well did you know him?'

'Only to look at. I mean, 'ow could you miss 'im? Better than most of them birds around here, as thin as sticks or great blobs, like fat-stuffed Frenchies. I mean, he was tasty he was. Right tasty.' Luciana widens her eyes. 'Nah mate, I'm not saying I'm a steamer, y'know, not into dick am I? Just being a private dick, innit, princess?

'If you live around the Portobello you gotta be able to appreciate the good stuff, whatever it is. Otherwise, you might as well poke fingers in your own two eyes.'

'E vero, true,' says Luciana. Trev grins with pleasure. 'I always liked the good stuff,' he continues, 'never knew why. Don't matter though. I reckon the good stuff sort of tells you. Up to you if you want to know what it's saying and why.'

Is he being too cool about Richard Metcalfe? I ignore my suspicions because I want to force out of him what he fancies in the markets. What makes his heart race in Portobello Road, I wonder out loud. Is it Georgian silver or Edwardian books, Victorian jewels or Byzantine icons? Maybe Chinese porcelain or French marble busts? Cartier watches . . . Cuban film posters?

'He doesn't know enough to know,' Luciana interrupts.

Her barb is well aimed. I'm being pompous and

pushy. I shrug and smile a sort of apology at Trev.

I pick up the photographs I think are most important and put the first of them on the table.

'Ok, let's have a summary, shall we? I'll start by telling you what I see. Then you tell me what I've missed.'

'I'll tell you what you missed right now, mate,' says Trev.

Chapter 11

●

Trev strides across the room, still unsteady on leather soles, picks up the discarded envelope from the chesterfield and feels inside it. He pulls out stapled sheets of paper, folded and so smaller than the prints.

'This is what you're missing. Pathologist's report. No point trying to work out what them pictures mean when some geezer's already done that.'

Luciana and I nod agreement, shamefaced. 'Anyway, how come you got this stuff?' Trev asks.

'That's not the question we ask, remember?'

'If you don't ask . . .'

'You have to know when . . .

'What if I don't tell you stuff you need to know because you didn't ask?'

I gather the rest of the images, dump them onto the dining table, pull out the extra leaf it has at each end. 'Come on, let's all sit down and look at the same thing at the same time, and I'll tell you what the pathologist says.'

Luciana leans back in her chair and asks Trev the other question I wanted to ask.

'What's upsetting you, Trev?' It releases a flood.

'I've got feelings, innit! That's what! He's only a few years older than me.' His voice is tense and low. 'It makes you think, y'know, when you've seen other bad stuff. When you, when you know. . .'

Trev lifts a face contorted with conflict. 'I mean, there's not much difference is there? Between giving someone a bit of a smack for their own good and like doing real damage, like killing them or something. How do you know where that line is?'

'What, you mean if you're the evil bastard doing the damage?'

Trev tenses with defiance. 'Not just! It's the same on the other end, too.'

Pain clouds his eyes, pleading for help to understand something that bewilders him. He's making me understand something new. The danger line an attacker recognises might well be a million miles from the line a victim can't cross. Is that what he's saying?

Never thought of that before.

'What if the evil bastard doesn't know the difference between a smack in the face and . . . something worse?' Trev's repetition of the question brings no answer. He stops again and searches deep inside himself.

'And, if you are on the end of it, how do you know when being brave ain't enough, that it might be the end of you because you're being too brave?'

It'd be wrong to answer him.

'Well, you see it on the telly, innit? Them bad bastards never know how hard they've done someone. They don't hang around to clean up the blood or anything, do they? Them's not the ones what have to wait in the freezing cold for a night bus to a hospital because you ain't got no money for a taxi and them bastard ambulances slag off 'domestics' and won't come for hours . . .

'My old man never knew if he hit us too hard. Just hit, smashed, kicked and left. Moved on. Like he was changing TV channels or something.'

'He bashed your Mum?' I ask.

'I said! But when he come back a couple of weeks later there wasn't no signs left. So he did it again. Didn't think it had hurt much, but . . .' Trev hoods his eyes and turns his head over his left shoulder. He can't get away from what he's reliving.

'You, too?' I ask.

He's holding his breath, his head moving back and forth. He waits until he empties his lungs with a single blast through his nose. He turns to face us and shivers.

'Even when I was little, real small . . .' His voice is small, too, boyish and frightened. Should I ask him to tell us what he is seeing? Could we bear it?

Luciana reaches to put a hand on his shoulder. He jumps, but then relaxes, returning from his internal world to ours. Luciana locks on to his eyes.

'Is this too hard for you?'

'No. It's just that . . .' Anger reddens his face. He stamps one foot like an angry child might and utters a long, low growl. That loosens something. 'It's just, I know how much it hurts, how much he must have hurt. It makes me remember everything I . . .'

Luciana puts an arm around Trev that seems more than maternal. 'Those are very good reasons for finding his killer.'

After a long pause Trev says, 'I see that, I do.'

'I'll tell you what,' I say. 'Let's get rid of most of

those pictures. We don't need them now we've got the report, thanks to you, Trev.'

I scan the report, looking for what I judge the most relevant facts and select the photographs that best tell the story in the same order.

Then I scoop up the rest of the prints, stuff them back into the envelope and tuck that out of sight between the chesterfield's cushions again.

'OK, I think I know what this is all about now.'

'What? You mean whodunnit?' Trev asks, cocky again. 'The Deli-Detective strikes again,' he says, waving an imaginary flag.

'No. Nothing like that. I meant I've got a clear picture of each injury and its effect on him.' Luciana settles back in a chair, folding her arms, and Trev does the same.

'Better than I thought it might be,' says Trev. 'Can you imagine what someone might have planned with the knife and sausage filler?'

'I'd rather not,' I say and pick up the picture of Richard's bashed-in skull.

Chapter 12

'The first damage was this horrible injury to the left side of his head. That's where all the blood in his hair came from because it didn't kill him outright. You know how much head wounds bleed. His heart was still beating so the blood flowed and was soaked up by his hair for quite a while until it clotted.'

The gash in Richard's head is a crescent-moon shaped crater right through to the brain. Where the white skull protrudes through the mashed flesh it looks as though an animal has done the damage.

Below this the force used in the blow shattered a lot of the same side of his head. Where the scalp and hair were ripped away by its force the skull is as crazed as crushed eggshell. I point out a few thin white strands that twist in and out of the bone and clots. What are they?

Trev suggests someone might have tried to staunch the blood with a towel or something. We agree. So does the pathologist.

'That blow might not have killed him but it must have contributed at some stage.' Luciana has her arms outspread, her chin tightened and lifted, her shoulders raised. She looks like a cartoon of an Italian. It's hard not to laugh. I remind myself she has every right to look like an Italian.

My eyes are down as I answer her. 'According to the pathologist we'll never quite know. It's the second lot of injuries that seem to have finished him.'

I turn the first picture face down and then hold up a close-up of Richard's chest and abdomen. Long slashes start low, deep in the flesh and angle up towards his left shoulder and into his throat, becoming shallower as they do.

'These have been made in anger. Must have been when he was seated on the ground and resting against something. What else do they tell us?'

Trev shakes his head, but Luciana taps the image with the point of a red fingernail. 'There,' she says. 'Look at where the knife or whatever it was goes in. What are those smudges?'

The report has told me the answer. There's been blood flow after every cut except a very few. Not a lot but there would have been none if he was dead. He was alive when the slashing began.

Trev bounces in. 'You mean this is when he was killed?'

'Some of those cuts slashed arteries. He wouldn't be getting blood or oxygen in his brain after that.'

Luciana asks, 'Why slash so often and why would you slash him at all if you'd already bashed him that hard? Why not just hit him again?'

Bravo, Luciana. That is the big question in my mind too. The clue the pathologist gives is that the chest and neck wounds were done later than the head wound.

'So, it could have been some other person what done the shanking?' I know what Trev means but Luciana must ask.

'Cutting, stabbing,' he says. 'A knife is a shank. You

shank someone.' He gesticulates as though he has a knife in his hand, circling and feinting and lunging.

Luciana leans forward and slaps his hand. 'Typical,' she says and tosses her head with anger. 'Tough enough to carry a knife but can't call it by its proper name. Cowards!'

'Deliberate disassociation,' I say.

'Fantasy,' says Trev. 'That's how they walk away from their deeds with no conscience.'

'Deeds?' Luciana and I both want to know.

'Deeds. Like what heroes do.'

'I don't understand,' I say.

'You would if you was 15 and couldn't read or write. You don't leave home because you're frightened you won't get back because you can't read where the buses go or what the street signs say.

'That's why they make gangs and turn estates into castles that no-one else is supposed to enter. They think of themselves as heroes and defenders. They makes up words, invents rules, breaks rules and hurts people what don't play by their rules. They consider themselves righteous and that everything they do is justified, so crimes become deeds to be proud about.'

Trev's been very excited but now he is rigid and looking inward. 'But you're in a self-made prison and all you're protecting is your hopelessness. You'd never be a real hero or do proper deeds in the outside world.'

He's mumbling, freeing these words from somewhere profound. His change from 'they' to 'you' tells me he's no longer explaining but revealing his story.

'That feeling of being a hero in a castle is all you can call your own. And at the same time you are shouted at day and night by TV and posters and shops pushing stuff you'll never be able to buy like other people.

'If you want that stuff you has to thieve it. If you can't rob it, you deal drugs to make the cash. Be a prossie if you is a bird. No other choices, mate.'

Trev's long speech stuns me. Social insight is not what I expected.

'That's what I'd be like if I couldn't read or write,' he says with defiance. 'So would you. You ever think about that? Come on, tell the truth. You ever think what it'd be like not to read and write in the 1970s?'

Trev is making me angry. I'm giving him a leg up in life at the same time as trying to solve a murder out of a sense of justice. Why is he challenging my social awareness and conscience?

Luciana answers him before I can. 'No, I've never thought about it because I've never had to. But what I do know is that anyone who wants to be more than a fake knight in a fantasy palazzo can break out if they want to. If they have the balls. If he has the balls.'

She pauses long enough to encourage Trev to respond. As he opens his mouth she says, 'You did.'

Trev sucks in a huge sobbing breath, as though he's been stabbed. He slams his head into his chest and withdraws for so long I wonder if he's having a breakdown.

My mind seizes with the impossibility of ever knowing the truth of his pain and how many awful knots and scars there must be inside Trev for him to take so long to acknowledge and then to work out that it is safe to accept Luciana's compliment. To do that he has to admit a past and a journey that's very different from his current ambition to be a detective who makes great espresso.

I'd like to be more sympathetic but he's making me selfish and ratty. So far, my mission to discover everything about Richard Metcalfe has been taken up with learning about, well, listening to, lots about Trev. What a waste of time.

Or is it?

It's not. Trev has shown no-one is more able to understand Richard than him. He feels the pain of his death. He's far more likely to understand his life, too. Trev might discover Portobello perpetrators before Luciana and I could ever do.

When Trev looks up his eyes shine with such pleasure you'd swear there was a light bulb behind each golden iris. 'Thanks for getting me,' he says to Luciana. After a short deep breath, he turns to me. 'Better get on with it, Boss. Sorry to hold you up.'

'No problems, mate,' I say.

I pick up the next picture. It shows an extreme close-up of a chest wound from which fine tweezers are extracting something tiny and shiny. Is it plastic?

Chapter 13

●

'They found pieces of black plastic in some of the slash wounds,' I reveal. By the time those were made Richard was in a black plastic bag. Not a bin bag but a thick garden-rubbish bag. They're bigger and they'd need to be to put him into, even if he was folded in half.'

'Which he was,' says Trev. His fist is clenched and he's lunging it back and forth in long upwards strokes. 'Look. This is what you would do if you wanted to know what was in a black bag on the ground. You'd jab like this, wouldn't you, dig deep down and then pull it back up towards you and so the cut would be shallower as you finished each slash. Just like in them pictures.'

Luciana shudders and puts out her hand to stop Trev's illustration. He shrugs. 'You gotta make sure what you think is possible,' he says.

I agree with him. 'But I think there's something else,' I say. 'Perhaps whoever slashed like that didn't know he was in the bag. Or even that there was a body in there. That explains why there could have been a second person.'

'Or they might have wanted to check it was him,' says Luciana.

'Are we even sure it was the first attacker who put him into the bag?' Trev asks.

He's right. We can't take anything for granted but we agree to agree that the person who hit Richard on the head also put him in the bag.

'Someone with a big garden? Plenty of those around here.'

'Or it could have been one of them council workers what was sweeping the streets then.'

'I think that's something to forget until we run out of other ideas.'

Luciana is imagining the scene. 'So, someone might be slashing because they are angry at the bin bag. Fury and violence aimed at a bin bag. That's not normal.'

'It was for whoever did it. Perhaps it was somewhere unexpected?'

'But how horrible. To then find a body in the bag. I suppose that's when they stopped slashing.'

Luciana pushes back her chair. She walks up and down the sitting room, saying, 'Anger. Anger and then more anger. Anger made someone hit him and then there's more anger from someone slashing at a black bag. Who is that angry with Richard Metcalfe?'

'Anyone who's had sex with him,' Trev says.

'Because?' I ask.

'Because although it's fantastic and special to you, it's nothing to him and he might not even recognise you next time you see him.'

'You one of those?' asks Luciana.

Trev blushes. 'I told you, I'm not a steamer.' Luciana doesn't come back at him and he shakes himself out of his indignation.

'I don't just make coffee, you know. People talk and never think I'm listening. But I am and I'm learning. He was a real shit once he'd had you. Tons of people say so.'

This fits with what the costermongers have told me. They aren't passive to gossip but pursue it with their customers. It's their way of coping with the hum drum repetitiveness of bagging up apples and carrots outdoors all year round, either too hot or too cold.

Luciana circles the room again. 'Can we accept that the skull injury wasn't done in your kitchen?'

'The police found no signs of his blood there, except clotted in his hair where I found him . . .'

'Mate! Are you still using that table in the kitchen?' Trev is outraged.

'What do you think?'

'Don't know. That's why I'm asking, innit?'

I ignore his 'innit' this once and he turns to Luciana. 'I reckon someone was going to cut off his thing. Someone who was much angrier with him than the others. And what was that sausage machine about?'

'Getting complicated, Trev. Trouble with that is none of the people with a key seems that angry at Richard. I've asked them all and so have the police. Had good alibis too it seems.'

'Of course,' Trev says. 'That's the people you know have keys. What if there's some you don't know. Or someone who knows someone what knows someone with a key.'

'Like half of Portobello Rd . . . or more,' sniffs Luciana.

I tell Trev and Luciana to take time off. It's late in the afternoon and I've promised to reward their hard work with toasted bacon sandwiches, my way.

Grilled sweet-cure bacon and crunchy peanut butter topped with canned pineapple rings fried in butter until their sweet juices caramelise.

The secret is to start with the right ingredients and to treat them the right way. The toast must be good white bread, not the squashy sliced stuff but sliced from authentic bread, like the brick-oven loaves we sell from Justin de Blank's kitchens over by Harrods.

When they're toasted the slices mustn't lie flat and steam into pap but stand upright to crisp before being buttered. I wish more people knew that about toast.

Each sandwich has two tender layers of dry-cured bacon, the type that won't weep white stuff when it's cooking. The peanut butter should be as fresh as you can get and the crunchier the better. It gets slapped on to one side of the sandwich only.

And you must have a black pepper grinder.

When the pineapple slices are cooking in butter I watch until the sides begin to caramellise. Then I grind coarse black pepper on to them, and I prefer the fragrant peppercorns from Sarawak. The heat encourages the pepper's aromatic oils to open up and sing. Heat the black pepper longer than five minutes and the finest flavours and fragrances evaporate.

Grind some into a stew less than five minutes before serving and guests think you are a magician. When pepper is ground late onto cooked food you don't get the bonus. If it's not heated long enough there'll be fewer new flavour notes. That's true whenever you add pepper.

Yes, these are indeed more Dan's Deli-licious Gosh

Factors. I should write a book.

Caramellised pineapple with black pepper is a flavour combination I discovered somewhere in France. It sings anyway, but when you have a decent amount of caramellisation and get the black pepper right it's like opera in your mouth. I've even served the combo as a pudding, the peppered pineapple in cubes and then rolled in pancakes and topped with whipped cream flavoured with dark rum

When Trev sees the sandwiches, he laughs. 'You ever cooked for Elvis Presley, mate?'

He tells me Elvis loved bacon, peanut butter and banana sandwiches deep-fried in inches of butter. I make a joke gagging noise yet put the idea into my file of ideas for the future. But toasted not fried.

Cooking has given my mind the break it needed.

I go over where we are up to now. In essence, we know the problems and we need to do something about solving them. The enquiries will be shared between the three of us in clear areas. Less chance to overlap and duplicate I think – except that sometimes two versions of the same story are what make sense. But first we must agree on what we know and on what we need to know.

No blood flow on the dress, so he must have been attacked in his street clothes, and these have never been found.

Who stripped him and put him into the dress? Was this the same person who struck him? Was this before or after he died?

Oh, and whose dress was it anyway?

Trev stops eating and stands, wiping his mouth and face. 'I know what we done wrong!'

'With the sandwich?' I ask.

'No. We haven't thought about what's not there. It's something all the books leave out, Agatha Christie's Poyrot, them tough American private eyes, all of them. Y' know I said the telly leaves out too much stuff? This is the main one.'

He's rehearsing something in his head, checking he's right.

'Shit,' he mouths and seeing Luciana about to protest, he lifts his hand. 'No. Listen. When someone dies, all their . . . their stuff comes out. Well, yeah, their shit and their pee. That's how you tell someone is dead, not by putting a finger on their neck and turning to the camera and looking sad. But you never see it, do ya? Once you know this, all those TV shows and crime novels are fake. Fake because they never tell you about the smell of the shit and piss that slide out when you die.'

Luciana rips photographs from the envelope.

'He's right. That culo is clean. Someone washed him after he was dead. Well after. And cleaned the dress, too.'

'It would have been all over him if he was dirty when he was put in the bag . . .'

'Except he wasn't dead then, was he?' she adds.

'What does this mean?' asks Trev.

'That once he was dead, at least one person loved him and cleaned him, wanted to give him dignity in death,' Luciana says.

'Was this the same person who scented him, something else you can't see in photos,' I ask. 'Why would you put expensive scent on a body?'

'To hide the smell?' said Trev.

'Perhaps,' said Luciana. 'Perhaps. Or because you thought he would like it.'

'Or you loved him?' I suggest.

So, love for Richard rather than anger? That's fascinating but doesn't go anywhere near solving why he was taken to my kitchen. In a frock but with no underwear.

Chapter 14

●

Guy Fawkes Night, 1978, an hour later

As soon as the bonfire is hosed down, Freddy's steaming body is manhandled out by the braver guests and laid on the frost-crackled grass.

His mother Sherylene, known as Lena, has forced open the gate and run to him but is rushed inside, a room familiar to her, because she is hostess Meredith's charlady and known to most guests. Luciana is amongst these.

Meredith is American and is typical for being agog before titles. A princess is top social status for her. She's cool when Luciana flaps her Pucci kaftan (the designer is a marchese and a relative) and herds everyone else back inside, leaving me to see what I can before the police arrive. If they do.

Meredith is an East Coast bluestocking with the mandatory three names, short, thick bob of greying hair, summery blue eyes and metal-rimmed specs. Her usual patronising smirk of disdain has reappeared, an unsettling expression in any situation and unempathetic now.

I hear her lanky son Jem stop someone lighting a spliff. 'Not with the fuzz coming, man.'

My hair is twisted into a loose bun and fixed with incense sticks I picked from the head of a coral-studded brass Ganesha, the Indian elephant-God. I don't want strands to fall and muddy the forensics. Using two forks I pull back Freddy's jacket. Straw and ripped paper are padded between him and the cast-offs. That layer has been studded with chunks of white firelighters and the smell suggests there's been a sprinkling of fuel of some kind. Yet neither paper, firelighters nor fuel has ignited. Why?

It's hard to see because of lazy smoke from the logs of the fire. Here and there his clothes are singed but not charred by the bonfire, yet Freddy's face is unblemished by heat. I expected to see skin blistering at least because the flames had reached that high.

There are no signs of blood flow, but when I look further into his jacket, my body snaps upright as a stiletto point of ice races down my backbone, as agonising as a welder's fine flame might be.

Spine-chilling isn't just a lazy writer's turn of phrase. It happens.

I dare not believe what I've found about the body of the youth that steams and smokes before me. It begs questions but answers none.

Luciana brings me in a mug of mulled wine. I turn away to gulp it down, but its heat can't loosen my tongue.

My brain is aflame with images of what has happened to Freddy. Who has done what to him in the weeks since he disappeared?

When the police get there, it's my luck that Jeff is on Guy Fawkes Night duty because there are so many empty houses while folk go to watch bonfires. He hurries me into the back seat of a police car and, as I stop shaking and warm up, I get the words out to him, each one accompanied by ugly mental pictures of pain and abandonment.

Freddy resisted the flames because he was so cold, but his temperature is not because of the icy air of November.

The mysterious reflection that the fedora dislodged from his face was a mask of ice. The paper and fire-lighters and fuel had not ignited because his clothes were damp.

Freddy has been deep frozen.

Chapter 15

'Where's the list?' demands Trev.

'List? Of what?'

'The people at the bonfire party.'

Now that Freddy has turned up, Trev is besotted with discovering where he was between his disappearance during Carnival and Guy Fawkes night.

It's personal because Trev was at school with Freddy, has often sat in his mother's kitchen. Freddy's mixed race made him as isolated as Trev felt because of his father's abuse. Yet they'd not made the friendship Freddy had with Jem.

Like it or not we seem committed to working out what happened to Freddy. Two cases to solve when I'd prefer to have none.

Trev's right. I'd not, we'd not, done the basics. Without doing the work to discount those who were innocent, we'd not know who to count as suspects.

I roll a fresh sheet of foolscap paper into my Smith-Corona typewriter. I never tire of those sounds or the combined smell of the paper and the inky ribbon, and these are a starting pistol that fire up my thinking cap.

The real buzz is facing a clean sheet and not knowing if this is all you will do that day, or if the smacking of typewriter keys on paper will fill your ears. This time, I type at once.

Elgin Crescent, November 5th

Meredith Hall Lopez – hostess, American, 42
Jem Lopez – her son, only child, 17, UK born
Princess Luciana – born an Italian contessa, was married to a French prince; late 40s – ish
The Metcalfes – parents of Richard - 60s?
Kenny/Long John Silver – silver dealer – mid 20s
Araminta – dealer in vintage clothes, indeterminate age

I was there too but don't count. Neither does Freddy or his mother Lena, who was restricted to watch from the other side of the garden fence. She was in Meredith's house Monday to Friday as a char and would have been expected to be there the morning after Guy Fawkes Night to clear up but would never have been invited. That's why she was watching over the garden gate.

I don't expect Meredith asked how a single mother of a mixed-race boy coped with daily life and expressed racism, even though she was almost a single mother herself. Professor Diego Lopez, Meredith's husband and father of Jem, was never there but filled a tenured professorship in the United States. The difference between Lena and Meredith was size of income.

Luciana interrupts, bringing Detective Inspector Harding up from the shop. 'This is something of an informal, Dan,' he says, fiddling with the already oily Windsor knot of his tie. He glances with suspicion at Luciana and Trev.

'Trustworthy and tight-lipped,' I assure him.

The DI takes a while to process and accept this and then pulls prints out of his briefcase. We have seen them, the confusing pattern of letters and numbers scrawled in coloured sauces over the sinks of my basement kitchen. Once our convincing acts of surprise and shock are over, I ask him why he's showing us these.

'Frankly, none of my officers can do it?'

'Do what?' asks Luciana, not quite avoiding mockery.

'Can't read it,' says Harding.

'Aaaaah, not can't read. Not what I thought you meant.' Harding lets confusion wrinkle his face but being used to obstructive interviewees he continues. 'To be honest . . .

'I hope a Detective Inspector would always be honest!' Luciana hates anything but plain speaking.

I explain that Luciana is an Italian princess and has immense respect for British police officers. Her intent is to illustrate great expectations, not innate mistrust. My fingers are crossed.

'Ah, well, your ummm, princessness, aaah, well, someone in the station thought Dan might be the one to translate. You know, considering how you've helped in the past, Dan.'

'I think we'd be happy to have a go,' I say, including Luciana and Trev with a sweep of my arm.

The DI is wary and asks if we can guarantee secrecy. Reassured by three such looks of sincerity you'd trust

Jack the Ripper with your whoreish sister, he leaves us alone.

A thought occurs to me that should have been addressed long before. It's always the obvious that gets overlooked.

'You were there, Luciana. In the garden when Freddy was revealed. What else did you see?'

'Nothing special, I think . . .'

'Keep thinking.'

'Well, I was busy getting everyone inside.'

'Nothing unusual about anyone?'

'Don't think to. . . Except it was harder to get Jem in.'

'And?

'I suppose it was because he was crying. Suppose he didn't want others to see him.'

'Why crying?' I ask.

'Freddy were his best friend,' says Trev.

I turn away to wipe my eyes and then pick up the images of the writing on the wall.

'Any ideas?'

'We've got to know what they mean,' says Trev.

'Of course we do, that's the point, imbecille!'

'Don't get your knickers in a twist, princess! I get that. I mean we has to know the thoughts behind them.'

'Meaning?' I ask.

'First, whatever they are, the writer doesn't want to own them. Doesn't want to be associated.'

Luciana leans back, hands and eyes alive with admiration for Trev. 'Si, assolutamente, tesoro! If they did, they'd say what they meant. What you are saying is . . . '

'What I am also saying is, what it would be good to know . . . is . . . are these hate messages, are they blaming him? Or excusing themselves?'

These are very good thoughts, and we fall silent.

'I've thought of something else,' says Trev. 'Well, two.'

'Go on.'

'The person what wrote the messages doesn't have to be the one what left the knife. Even if it was, we can't trust they has anything to do with Richard.'

'You've watched too much television,' Luciana says but before Trev can take umbrage, she adds, 'It's just as well!'

I think of my detective friend Jeff. He can do The Times crossword just by looking at it. When I say I'll invite Jeff for supper, Luciana's eyebrow twitches and Trev's eyes open wide. Both want to ask something personal but a glare from me stops that.

The Permissive Society must know when something is none of its business.

Chapter 16

Banal to say so, I know, but complaints are like buses. After none for ages they come in a procession. Yesterday I had two, one about a pate and a stream about my orange cheesecake.

I didn't mind Lady Annunciata asking about my duck and orange pate. She wondered rather than criticised, asking if there might be more, well, more duckiness. I agreed. I've never solved the conundrum that a pork pate with a central layer of roasted duck breasts never tastes enough of them, not even using the collected French recipes of the sainted Jane Grigson.

Her ladyship offered no solution, accepting that fragility of supposed flavour was always a problem with a pheasant or grouse or duck pate. She mentioned it, flattering me, because she thought I might be able to solve the problem, a flavour failure that the French had never admitted.

'Don't tell them I said that,' she says, retaining her aristocratic accent even as she laughs. 'I suppose that's why our cooks pot our leftover roasted game birds, mashing the flesh with butter and spices. Such flavour.'

'Taste that, Dan!' interrupted a dumpy woman with violet hair wearing clay-spattered denim, a local craft potter.

'No, go on,' she insisted when I stepped back. She picked up a spoon used for serving olives, wiped it on her pinafore, scooped up orange cheesecake from the part-eaten slice she held, and pushed it towards my mouth. I avoided it but smeared a fingerful and tasted that.

'It's wrong, isn't it?' demanded the potter. 'It's different, it's boring and, excuse me for saying, I don't think you made it.'

'True, that is,' interrupts the Swedish baroness, shooing her blonde twins from the pastries beside Bella. 'My boys won't eat it anymore. Orange is not there.'

'But, it's my recipe, it must . . .'

'Been meaning to mention it, Boss,' said Jeremy. 'Quite a few complaints and returns . . . '

I'm shocked. Complaints about orange cheesecakes, one of my star creations?

'The passion isn't there, is it? You are getting bored,' insists the potter.

This accusation digs deep. My cooking means everything to me but it is not my passion. It's cranky and grumpy, I know, but I have an aversion to those who declare 'passion' for anything, food in particular.

'Passionate' cooks are forever offering me pickles and pies and cakes, breads, pastries and mustards, jams and jellies, hoping we will stock them. Most sound good but fail to deliver flavour, all of them creations of fine phrases rather than flavour.

I call this cooking for the plate rather than for the palate, for looks not tastes.

The palate detectors of my customers are right. The cheesecake hasn't been made in my kitchen for weeks. A professional caterer who is a neighbour and customer asked if she might bake for us. She cooks private dinner parties, including for serious royalty, but said she had capacity so I asked if she would take over the orange cheesecake; its long cooking time clogs up my ovens now Christmas is close. As well as capacity for our pizzas, pates and such, there are Christmas mince pies and basins of puddings with pre-decimal silver coins in them. They're steam-baked in foil-sealed trays of water, my version of steaming in pots.

When I tell Mrs Cheesecake she's lost the job because of complaints about the orange cheesecake she has greater concern for her reputation than for mine or what she might be doing wrong.

• • •

November 12th, 1978

It's a week since Freddy steamed on the Guy Fawkes bonfire, and this Saturday is the first time most locals can treat the shop like an ancient village pump. They gossip while buying, making it easier for anyone serving to add an extra weight of cheese, ham or German calves' liver sausage. Few care when asked for agreement, and extra weight means extra income and that soothes my feet, which scream to be in sandals rather than boots.

Many would have known Freddy by sight, and all craved the sharing of outraged revulsion.

'I know! Only 17 . . .'

'Yes, and, well, mixed . . . '

'Not many of those, not yet.'

'Nice way of saying it!' My customers shuffled and coughed as they wondered how to describe Freddy.

'That's right. White mother, Caribbean father.'

'Not the other way?'

'Unlikely, dear. Not a white father and a . . . Oh no.'

There is a lot of that.

Dan's Deli is on Portobello Road almost on the corner of Elgin Crescent, which marks where the Saturday 'antique' market becomes a fruit and veg market that's there Monday to Saturday. Elgin Crescent is thought a border by many. Other than Portobello Road, most areas north or east of the crescent are dismissed as British West Paddington, the way our rulers named a colony in Africa or the Caribbean.

White folks might go northwards up Portobello Road as far as the Westway viaduct but the further they go the less they veer into the streets either side of Portobello. Colville Terrace is opposite smart Elgin Crescent yet was where I first saw landlady signs saying: No dogs, no irish, no BLAKS.

My older customers are the most tolerant of such change. Mrs Andrews is over 80 and as tiny as you could imagine yet she'd saved me from a knifeman last year. A drug-disturbed youth didn't like me refusing to give him a bottle of wine on credit. The rebuffed Hon. Toby picked up a knife and held it inches from my chest. Ten or so people in the shop froze, as did I. I won't repeat what he called me.

Into this impasse of solid but spineless W11 citizens

strode wee Mrs Andrews, saying, 'Oh we don't want that sort of nonsense in here. Go away. Go home.'

He shuffled off at once, back to his noble but disinterested family and was never seen again.

This time, she piped, 'I thought Freddy was very handsome and what was he, just 17?'

Not expecting an answer, she asked for her weekly slice of farmhouse pate and a big wedge of unpasteurised Brie de Meaux, voted King of Cheeses at the 1814 Congress of Vienna.

'The only place you can get this outside Harrods,' she adds, winking and knowing this puffery always meant extra sales for me and generosity to her.

The hunger for outrage resumes.

'You know he was frozen?'

'That's why he was steaming.'

'He was. Melting into his clothes.'

'Not his clothes, I heard. Too smart.'

'Who knows? Mind you, he disappeared months ago, Carnival weekend, wasn't it?'

'I've been told the clothes belonged to Diego . . .'

'What? Meredith's hubby?'

'Her char told me she burns his old clothes regularly.'

'Who, Lena, who does me on Tuesday?

'That's her. Says Meredith burns them, yes.'

'But, not on a corpse, surely!'

'No, she says he hates the idea of someone else in his pants!'

'Better than the other way!'

'That's not what . . .'

'Ghastly, that idea of wearing second-hand. Nightmare.'

'Big business down past the fruit and veggie market.'

'And how would I know that?'

Most accents are Establishment or try to be. Between here and back up the hill to Notting Hill Gate via Portobello Road or up smarter Kensington Park Road that runs parallel, there are many rich single addresses, often lived in for generations. Titles, war heroes, scions, Trust rather than State beneficiaries, famous actors and actresses. Writers and artists aplenty.

They mix my shop floor with those who clean or nanny for them, or who shiver in digs longing for recognition, stardom or a few more Johns to buy dope or themselves.

The many Saturday shop assistants managed by Jeremy include an ex-Vogue model, a couple more from the estates and plenty of colonials. There's someone for everyone to identify with or to patronise.

'Of course,' says a blimpish old man with a preposterous moustache, who buys nothing but Stilton and Bath Oliver biscuits. 'There's a lot of ignorance there. Indians y'know.'

'No Indians involved!' shouts an outraged young woman in muslin, beads and sandals. 'And how dare you call them ignorant?'

'Not Indians themselves, m'dear. Their customs. Burnin' bodies, don't y'know. Saw it everywhere, Indian Army for years.'

I intervene. 'What's your point, Colonel?'

'Takes hours. You'd never get away with murder by burnin' a body on a pesky little British bonfire. Bandage-wallahs reckon each cremation takes close to half a ton of dry wood. Surprised India's got any trees left . . .'

At last. A clue to solving Freddy's murder. The Guy Fawkes' bonfire wasn't part of a well-laid scheme but an ignorant amateur hoping to destroy evidence of a murder.

That narrows it down to most locals.

'Very interesting, Colonel,' I say. 'What's more important is who did it. Anyone heard anything?'

'How about you, Dan? You must know something.'

I tell them I know nothing. What I know about Freddy's body is being kept to myself.

On top of the images of Richard's corpse, details of Freddy the Fire are getting to me. I've had enough of dead bodies and what horrid people have done to them.

Nothing's been solved about Richard. Now Freddy has turned up after going missing during the Carnival in August. My mind is as snappy as a Jack Russell at a burrow. But one thing at a time. I should be concentrating on Christmas. If a deli doesn't do well at that time, it'll be out of business during winter's lean months.

Even so, I retrieve the prints of the curious edible writing that was on my kitchen wall when I discovered Richard Metcalfe's body. As far as I can make out they are something like:

OTI473M515Th216
pvb1012but . . .
MMY Compz4comp

If the messages seek to explain or defend, why are they so opaque? It is either a deliberate diversion by a clever mind, or it's the fantasising of a broken mind that's crystal clear to itself but impenetrable to us.

Are they codes? If they are codes, are they the work of a broken mind or of a clever-dick mind? I sit up. Clever-dick? Brilliant! Golden Dick/clever dick. Is that the connection? Maybe it is, but it's too bloody clever for me to understand.

My detective friend Jeff said some police whizzes were given a couple of hours to work on them but came up with nothing. Their best inspiration was to treat the figures and numbers as co-ordinates on maps, but then they had to search through dozens of Atlases and street guides plus the six-digit Post Codes introduced four years ago. So they didn't. Makes you feel safe, doesn't it?

Just for the hell of it I get out my biggest edition of London A to Z and retreat to the depths of the bean bag. Sometimes we don't see what we should because it's too simple, too much under our noses.

When I wake up 45 minutes later it's my nose that's under the book. Luciana and Trev are standing over me.

They remind me those people at the Guy Fawkes party must be interviewed. Also, that we don't even know why Richard was wearing a red dress.

Luciana, Trev and I agree our targets and promise to keep me up to date.

With the Christmas rush getting closer, it will be too easy to overlook something important.

Or someone.

PART TWO

METHOD

September 14th to December 24th
1978

Chapter 17

•

September 14th, 1978

The Metcalfes have been sabotaging our efforts to talk to them about their son when either has been in the shop, so Luciana and I mount a joint confrontation.

A gutsy southerly wind makes walking up the Portobello hill a chore. On a weekday in autumn there are few lights in shop windows, no street stalls and no arcades open, so I feel uncomfortable and vulnerable. Well behind us, just a few costermongers have set up their stall, as they must.

I'm grateful for my fleece-lined Afghan coat, even though my heat and the outside dampness together encourage reminders of what once lived inside it.

Luciana is cosy in a bottle-green, triple-ply cashmere twin set and Donegal tweed trousers. On top she's wrapped a post-box red, full-skirted coat in thick wool.

'Givenchy,' she tells me, '1954.' She checks the huge black buttons are each doing their job. And then that her Arctic fox pillbox hat is firmly pinned.

I'm hoping Luciana might make Johnny Metcalfe feel secure enough to tell us something we don't know. He worships what her titles stand for, a world of order with everyone in their allotted and contented place, as he sees it.

It takes a long time to get the door answered. There's a shallow porch but the cold wind makes it uncomfortable to huddle even there and Luciana wants to leave. I press the doorbell a third time leaving my finger on it for a count of five.

Belinda erupts from the door, takes stock for a few seconds, and then knocks between our ankles with a busy broom, shooting debris from the doorway and footpath into the gutter.

She's not happy to see us yet has applied scent, something citric that makes me think of Earl Grey tea. Her unpainted mouth looks like the tied-off end of a salami.

'He's not very well,' she mutters, and then her face softens. 'But I know he'd like to thank you for being kind the other day. In the shop.'

It was horrible. Johnny couldn't count out the coins in his palm. I came down to the shop to find him red and defensive while Jeremy added up silver from his trembling palm.

Everyone else in the shop stared, few with sympathy. I got him upstairs, where he burst into sobs. By the time I'd made tea he was calmer but still shocked.

'It's getting worse, not better,' he mumbled. 'Worse. Not right, old man. Not able to count money . . .'

I made as light as I could and once he seemed capable I took him down the stairs and gave him the shopping that Jeremy had put to one side.

On Portobello Road he dithered about which was the way home. I watched until he found his blood-red door up the hill, between two antique shops that open at indeterminate times during the week, one selling maps and globes, the other dealing in silver of all periods and qualities.

Belinda lets us in through that same shiny door and leads us up a narrow tunnel of a staircase enclosed against one wall of the silver shop. Like the door, the ceiling and walls are of blood-red gloss paint and the stairs are carpeted to match. Magnificent old flintlock rifles with intricate, inlaid stocks hang high. It's an artery of armoury.

Among the rifles are sheathed daggers on brass-studded belts. Some have curved blades, and many are inlaid with flat-topped lasques or studded with rose-cut diamonds and bubbles of cabochon sapphires or rubies. Pin-point lights reflect luminous patterns back on to the red paint.

The Khyber Pass was never like this.

The sitting room on the first floor overlooks Portobello. It's bright with light from tall, sash windows and is over-stuffed with empty echoes of a life that won't be seen again. I bet a British officer's club in Poona during the Raj looked like this.

Framed sepia photographs sweep over every available surface. Most feature men in uniform, sometimes with bejewelled maharajahs or other Indian notables, and with dead animals or hunting trophies displayed afoot. Rolls-Royce shooting brakes and bi-winged planes feature.

The walls are a rich gold and smothered with more photographs, prints and oils, all of them exotic but haunting and empty at the same time.

A lamp on a carved-teak desk has a pierced brass shade and a beaded fringe and the air is thickened with the resonance of woody incense and wisps of smoke from the flames in the grate of a Victorian tile-surrounded fireplace.

The desk and all about it are piled with antique-trade magazines and newspapers, many with holes scissored or torn into them. There's another pile of scrap books in which the snipped articles are catalogued.

Johnny slumps like a tipped-out mousse in an armless, buttoned-velvet chair close to an opened window. He's wiping tears from his eyes and doesn't conceal this.

When he sees Luciana, he struggles to stand. She puts out her hand and leans over him insisting he stays seated. He falls back, his eyes welling.

'Still a bit tough is it, Johnny?' I ask.

'On top of everything else it is, old boy, yes.' I query this with a puzzled face. He waves a hand. 'That business in the ummm, your . . . sorry, old boy. No, can't get the word. Not up to standard, is it? Frustrating but y'know, that place you've got. What's it called . . . ?'

'He's not well . . .' Belinda speaks into my ear, just above a whisper. Johnny shakes his head and then waves a trembling hand. I think he's still trying to find and say 'deli'. Belinda takes his gesture as permission to speak on his behalf.

'It's more than Richard you know. It's . . .' She too wants to say more but starts at a movement by Luciana, who has gone to a spindle-legged bamboo table supporting an old-fashioned black telephone with a round dial.

Luciana picks up a folded card and holds it up to me. It's for hospital appointments. I can see the department it's from.

'Radiology?' I ask.

'Over now,' Belinda says.

Of course. How stupid of me. Being unable to count money and getting confused about direction don't mean Johnny's going ga-ga. Neither do his other symptoms.

I tot up the evidence. Johnny's weight gain, difficulty finding words, losing his sense of direction, loss of numeracy, his obvious depression - and sitting by an opened window when it's freezing outside.

'Is it prostate cancer?' I ask. Johnny nods. 'You're on hormone therapy, aren't you, Johnny?'

His eyes bubble and mine flow with burning tears, too. There's my bloody over-burden of empathy again.

Chapter 18

Hormone therapy means testosterone suppression. It's when men share with women the worst of body-changing experiences. Some men sail through, just as some women give little note to the 'change'.

There's a rush of anger in me. Male hormone suppression has been common since the 1940s if you have prostate cancer but it's often unnecessary and the costs of the potential side-effects seem little understood by those who administer it.

Even when suppression is stopped, it can be a life sentence because there is no guarantee that natural testosterone production will begin again. Oncologists are terrified testosterone replacement will stimulate more tumours. So they don't replace it, sentencing thousands of men to a life of unwarranted mental turmoil and sexual impotency.

Johnny and I agree on this unkindness. Recurrence can be monitored with simple blood tests.

Belinda and Luciana are shaken and uncomfortable. Women don't expect to hear men complaining about hormonal changes and hot flashes. They are flushes, not flashes, in my opinion.

'I suppose they tell you it's 'just' depression. Is that right, Johnny?'

He nods. His eyes are still filled with tears. Helplessness and shame did that to me, too.

'Was the tumour very big?'

Belinda answers for him.

'Not really.'

As I thought. Johnny is over-medicated and over-treated with no interest in the effects this has on his quality of life. Or on anyone else's, except for a doctor's tally of treatments.

'Hardly a man, old boy. Not even a man . . .' He lifts his head and bores silent meaning into me. It's a sign of how low he is that a man of his convictions would dare raise this with Luciana and Belinda in the room.

'You see what they've made me,' Johnny asks. 'For a tumour you couldn't find on a pin head.'

Johnny lifts his left hand. It holds a small, thick book with a leather cover. 'Know what I am? I'm a eunuch. Men not considered fit to enter a church.'

I see it now. The book is a bible. Plenty of people with no quality of life from medicine turn to religion.

Belinda puts an arm around Johnny. 'That's enough. You can see what talking about it does. And then there's his heart, that's not good at all.' I understand, but now we are in the house I must achieve more.

Bless Luciana. She's taken off her coat, picks up some signed photographs and engages Johnny, establishing they know maharajahs in common.

'Can I, might I, have a look at Richard's bedroom?' I ask Belinda.

'The police did that,' she says.

'Did they find anything interesting?'

'Not that they told me.'

'Well, may I? I'll tell you what I'd like to find. A diary or a notebook, something with dates, times . . .'

'He was too clever for that.' There's sneaking pride in her tone. It's a chink of light into her dead son. Can I push that door wider?

'What do you think he did instead?'

'About what?'

'Well, keeping records of his dates and his . . . conquests, I suppose you'd call them.' Her back straightens.

'Very exaggerated. The way people talk you'd think he'd seduced every young girl within five miles.'

'Had he?' I ask. From what I know that's very possible. And a great number of boys, women and men, too.

Belinda shakes her head and sucks her lips until they disappear.

Richard's bedroom is untidy but that's because the police have been here, looking for fingerprints or other clues. Yet, it was neither the den of a slob nor the antiseptic retreat of a minimalist. It's bland and I think this is planned.

The walls and every piece of furniture in the room are an elegant grey, French grey is it? The blinds and curtains match, as does the plain carpet. It seems a deliberate antidote to the sitting room's mausoleum of memories.

It's also no competition for Richard Metcalfe, a monotone background that would champion his beauty.

'Were you allowed in here,' I ask Belinda.

'He was a teenager. Hated me in here. He kept it tidy enough, so I agreed never to come in.'

'Was he allowed to bring friends back?'

'Not to his bedroom.'

Belinda slams her hands on to her hips and stands less than a footstep from me. 'Look, why don't you drop the questions?' She waits for an answer, but I give her none. 'It's a job for the police,' she continues, 'and the more you interfere, the harder it is for Johnny and for me to get on with our lives.'

'But he was murdered! Abandoned rather than being buried like some stray animal. Richard is your son and he's been taken. Don't you want to punish whoever did those horrible things?'

Belinda's eyes narrow. 'I think the people who did it are suffering anyway. Can you imagine being driven to do such things? You'd regret it, wouldn't you? Perhaps that's punishment enough?'

Oh dear. Sympathising with the murderer. Not a good sign, even though I know this is one of my traits.

I'm trying to formulate a sensible response when there's a cry from the sitting room. Johnny has fallen. Belinda flies downstairs leaving me a bit peeved. I might have steered her anger deeper into Richard's world.

My nose twitches at the trail of scent Belinda has left. There's something arresting about it that won't leave me. What was bright and citrussy on the doorstep is now like a damp garden. Why is my stomach contracting?

I close my eyes so my brain can range free. And then I get it. The red dress. This is the same but with fresher notes than the chypre scent someone had put onto Richard in my kitchen. My heart races as I assess the significance. But not for long.

Nothing, it means nothing I decide. If Richard had borrowed the dress from his mother why wouldn't he borrow her scent, too?

This is wasting stolen minutes in the boy's room. I'll be expected to follow Belinda. I slide open the nearest wardrobe.

Richard's not been prissy about his shoes. They are tumbled together at the bottom of the closet. He had dozens of pairs, many of them handmade or hand finished, lined with satin-thin leather and stamped with iconic St James's and Mayfair labels. There are hundreds of pounds worth when new, but I know you can pick up used pairs for a few quid or less at the junkier Golborne Road end of Portobello's Saturday Markets.

As I turn the shoes over, I hear a metallic rattle. It's a familiar sound but I can't place it. Then, one brown lace-up brogue is heavier than it should be. Inside I find a spray can of anti-fog, the stuff that keeps car windows clear in winter. I shake it to check. Yep, that's the rattle identified and this tells me what else to look for.

It's too easy. I discover cotton buds when I find the matching shoe. Now I have to prove my hunch is right.

Why did he hide anti-fog and cotton buds among his shoes, even though his mother wasn't allowed in his room? I think I know. Richard was so noticeable in public he must have valued privacy. He created secrets in the isolation of his bedroom even though none was needed.

I blow on each of the room's mirrors. One shows results. I'm right. Richard Metcalfe used cotton buds and demister for invisible writing. His breath on the mirror would reveal it.

There's a single address and a date, nothing else.

Is this where and when he wore the red dress?

Chapter 19

Johnny has been settled back into his chair and seems relaxed. Yet there's a begging in his eyes. Belinda takes a bottle of scent from a drawer in the carved teak desk and sprays it in the air close to him. It's the one she put on before opening the door to us. It seems too expensive to spray into the air. She senses rather than sees my surprise.

'Scent. Smell. One of the few things that give Johnny pleasure. It goes straight to the oldest part of our brain you know.'

Ah yes, I do know. During my prostate-cancer treatment I went to gardens to breathe old-fashioned roses. They inspired a sense of serenity and optimism when none existed. I scented my pillows and bed linen with rosewater and sought out attar of roses, the distillation of natural rose oil popularised by Noor Jahan, mother of Shah Jahan

My earlier impression is wrong. It's not woody incense lingering in the air, it's notes of the scent that linger. It startles a discomforting image of Richard's abandoned body in my kitchen.

Belinda tells me it's Clinique's Aromatic Elixir.

'Very disturbing,' says Luciana. 'Exotic but inter-sex and hippie with its patchouli, a little floral somewhere and quite green and wet. The best of many worlds. Also the worst.'

In the awkward silence this creates, Johnny offers us a drink but we decline and Luciana kisses his cheeks goodbye. Belinda leads us back down the scarlet tunnel of arms.

I stop halfway. I must use every second, no matter how insensitive it seems. 'Oh yes. That red dress, Belinda.'

'He wore it to a party. A Tarts and Vicars party. That's where he was going.'

'What? He went as a Tart rather than as a Vicar?'

'Wouldn't you if you looked like him?' she snaps.

Belinda's anger is back but I'm comfortable enough to confront it. 'What, go dressed like a woman, rather than as a man?'

'Richard knew he'd always be the centre of attention and invite jealousy or mockery. So he played to it. Played up to it. Called it his Colosseum default. Pandering to the mob by letting them have his blood without a fight.'

'Blood? Do you think someone at the party . . .?'

'Figure of speech. As you well know, Mr Heath!' Belinda's ire might just allow something vital to slip out. I keep up the pressure.

'I take it he borrowed it from you.'

'A dress like that? In that colour? Certainly not!'

'Then where . . .'

'Meredith, I expect. His friend Meredith. Or one of the second-hand stalls on Saturdays? It was some smart couturier. Rahvis, I think the label said. That's what Meredith deals in. Exclusive names like that.'

'Sisters in Mayfair, that's who Rahvis is,' Luciana adds. 'Very expensive, even second hand. No two the same.'

'He didn't work, did he? Where would he get the money?'

'Who knows? He did deal you know. Like Johnny and I have always done.'

'What? You all deal marijuana?'

'That's insulting! Richard didn't even drink. He said his mind was too beautiful.' She waves an arm. 'These, these guns and knives, that's what he dealt in. Started with a piece we gave him when he was 12. He made money from them, must have, some of these are worth thousands. More than that . . .'

'Did you see him in the dress?'

'Of course. Fabulous, of course,' she says. I take a twitch of her mouth to be a smile but it's hard to know if it's broad or regretful.

'Who gave the party?' Luciana asks.

'No idea.' Her tone is colder. 'But he could walk there, even in those heels.'

Neither knows that I might have found where the party was, thanks to the mirror writing in Richard's bedroom.

'Did he have a credit card, cheque book?'

'Cash only with Richard. He hated people having records of his life.

'A bank account?'

'Not that I knew.'

'Any money in his room?'

'The police found a few coins.'

Her voice falls away and her eyes drop to introspection. She moves off the bottom step and opens the door for us, at once kicking away a shard of paper and a cigarette butt.

'That was the last time I saw him alive . . . it was here. . .' Belinda is holding the door open and gulping back sobs she cannot control.

We twist to brush past her and step onto Portobello Rd.

I want to hold and comfort her, but I also want to run away from sharing her misery. Most of all I want an end to the mystery of Richard's death and, if Belinda's weeping exposes a new truth, I might get a helpful clue.

'That's all . . . that's all I can tell you.' Her eyes are fixed far, far away. She holds her hands over her face, shakes her head and then turns and closes the door.

The world that took her son is locked out and then chained again and again.

'Il prezzo. Il prezzo della bellezza . . .' Luciana is as pained as Belinda but far from tears. I know her locked down expression. She's thinking. I know she's rueing 'the price of beauty' but not why. She'll explain when she is ready. In the meantime, she says, 'So. Richard knew Meredith. Wonder where that will lead?'

'Silence reigns, at last!' A voice interrupts from the next shop door.

A tall and flimsy man in his 20s blows an exaggerated plume of smoke and rolls his eyes. He's standing outside his silver shop, although standing is not quite the word. He's folded against it, his legs twisted one more time than most of us can manage. I think Yogists call it The Snake. It'll be no surprise to learn he's known as Long John Silver. His lips are pursed in the pregnant way of any gossip with something urgent to tell.

'The noise! Talk about cats on heat. Day and night they were at it . . . to be honest, I was relieved when he went missing. Shouldn't speak ill of the dead and all that, I know, but I say as I sees and there's no harm in that . . .'

'No idea what you mean.' Luciana wants him to get on.

'Weeks it was. Day and night.'

'How do you know about nights? Do you sleep in the shop?'

'Best time to change prices, do teeny stock takes, that sort of thing, darling. Far too busy during the day.'

Luciana looks up and down the deserted street. 'Yes, I can see that.'

It's my turn. 'So, this fighting? Who?'

'That Richard and his mother and father. And throwing stuff.'

'About what, the fights I mean?'

'Couldn't hear everything. You know how thick the carpets are.'

I do. The Metcalfe's floor is carpeted but that's smothered by oriental rugs and one of the biggest tiger skins I've seen. It might even be a white tiger. I correct myself. Might have been a white tiger.

His lips purse again and he too looks up and down the street. He giggles. 'But that stairwell picks up everything, magnifies every sound, like a trumpet or something.'

'Like when you put a glass to it?' Luciana's interruption causes an enormous appeal to the heavens. When his eyes return to their proper place, he leans forward. 'It's fibre board,' he whispers. He waits for Luciana to respond but she just nods, as though complicit.

'Anyway,' Long John continues leaning back, 'you'll know I'm not one to gossip but the language! F this, F that you F-ing this and . . .'

'And no idea what it was about?'

'Fucking! That's all I heard. And useless. That's the word I heard most, apart from all the fucking, I mean.'

Given Richard's propensities I'm not surprised at the subject. But I am surprised at Belinda and Johnny . . . it seems out of character.

'There was the other one, too. Much goings on there . . .'

'Other one?'

'That pushy American one, who deals in old frocks. A real potty-mouth, that one.'

Luciana and I lock eyes. Meredith. Again.

The wind is less aggressive on our backs as we turn to walk down Portobello Road. Long John Silver calls after us.

'That business with the broom? Don't take it personally. She's hysterical about anything on the doorway. Stupid cow.'

With that he unfurls himself and slams his door, laughing with an excitement I put down to his pleasure in sharing his self-important observations.

Chapter 20

Bella's coffee and hot milk fragrances are sneaking out into the street to greet our cold noses by the time Luciana speaks.

'Il prezzo!' She growls out the two words again, just as Puccini's fated Tosca does when bargaining with Scarpia for her lover's life in Castel Sant'Angelo. Luciana's voice stays low and portentous.

'The cost of losing beauty is higher than of owning it.'

'What opera is that from?' I ask. It's a mistake. She stops and plants herself in front of me. Her big blue eyes are icy.

'Why is a good thought or a clever phrase always expected to be by someone else? I made it up. Me. I said "The cost of losing beauty is even higher than of owning it." Then. On the spot. '

Her eyes change in an instant. They're warm and sparkling again. 'And you can quote me on that.'

She's put me in place and now takes my arm before we cross Portobello, returning a wave from Fred and his son Tony through the windows of Kingsland Butchers, our neighbours and a centre of much amusement to Portobello shoppers. They only gut chickens when they are bought. Fred throws each one to Tony over customers, shouting 'D-rib flying'. They use much back slang and disturb shoppers by asking if they prefer a big cock when selling pheasants and grouse. I never see that shop empty.

Back upstairs I consider the challenge of emotion having no place when investigating murder because it hauls you into too many blind alleys. But this bloody over-empathy thing I've got! It means not just understanding how someone else feels but feeling it with them. I'm quite as distressed over the distress of Johnny and Belinda as I am about the murder of their son.

Empathy to this degree leaves little emotion over for me. I want my emotions back, to be mine again. That's becoming the main reason I want to solve the murder of Richard Metcalfe. I don't care if that is selfish.

By the end of the day Luciana has agreed to sniff around the many places Richard might have bought or borrowed the dress. It's strange that no-one has asked about it or claimed something for its loss.

Trev is now a qualified barista and hard to get away from his listening post at Bella. As well as the gossip he overhears from those who forget he is there, he can see a good stretch of Portobello Road and down into Elgin Crescent and is aware of what goes on and who walks past.

Once the deli is closed and I'm full length over the lumps in the chesterfield, Belinda's last words keep coming back. "That's all . . . that's all I can tell you . . ."

Did she mean she was too exhausted to say anything more?

Or she isn't permitted to say more? Or doesn't she dare?

It's upsetting how often I know the right questions

when it's too late to ask them. Is it stupidity, or does my mind need extra time to absorb and process facts these days? It's obvious now that Belinda Metcalfe's mini-mouth is not telling me all it could.

I wonder why?

I'm falling asleep but think of something else. I bet the same is true about stringy Long John Silver, too.

Where did Richard keep his money?

And why did Belinda say the doorway was the last time she saw him alive? Might she also have seen him there dead?

Or in a black bag?

. . .

It's time I explain Jeff, the young, plain-clothes detective sergeant from Ladbroke Grove police station, the bloke who can do The Times crossword without writing in the boxes. We met in the deli and at once liked one another in the wordless, visceral way that happens but is unexplainable.

Jeff's interest in new cheeses was infectious and he appreciated the time I spent sharing samples when there was something new from the White Van Men.

This expanded into evenings at mine where we trialled new taste pairings. Wax-textured honeycomb honey with bleu de Bresse, that soft one with streaks of blue, was a revelation. Suave was the word we agreed, not a million miles from drinking a sauterne or a port with Stilton, yet with none of the piercing acidity of that cheese and with the extra chew of the beeswax. Yes, suave. We were pleased with that.

One night, while struggling to identify why Yorkshire's early forced rhubarb and red Cheshire cheese have no affinity, he stood and asked if he could stay and sleep with me.

'I won't touch you,' he added. 'And you'd better not do anything.'

Jeff is from Cumberland, part of Cumbria since 1974, and Notting Hill is a long way from there he'd said. His family and their home had been poor and so he had always shared a bed with a brother.

'I miss that feeling of, I dunno, I suppose of belonging and feeling secure. You know what I mean?' I didn't know but it made sense Jeff and I might do one another good.

I had always wanted a brother and I felt it could be strengthening to have an intimate and trusting connection with another man. So, we began to sleep together from time to time, which seemed to ground us both. Jeff always left early yet somehow Luciana and Trev know and must think we are at it.

We aren't but there is random spooning. It isn't mentioned and I never resist.

Tonight, Jeff is entranced by the symbols from my kitchen wall. Like crossword sleuthing but with a point, he declared. First, he copies them out, one on each of three quarto sheets and all the while I see his incisive mind working as he pauses to think, nod and then continue.

OTI473M515Th216

pvb1012but . . .

MMY Compz4comp

Jeff takes the last one first, saying he'd recognised

the initials MMY as Mahareshi Mahesh Yogi, the guru who introduced Transcendental Meditation to the West in the 60s, helped by the Beatles.

'He said a very few wise things and hundreds that are senseless. An uppity uniformed sergeant said this one to me a couple of days ago. Competition is for the competent.'

'Meaning?'

'Nothing. An empty put down. Can't see the relevance here . . . although might it mean . . .'

'. . . what, that Richard was playing a game that was beyond him?'

'Or that the person who wrote didn't understand his game. Could be jealousy, of course. Or a silly brag.'

Jeff moves on and says nothing for some time until he spells out the next one.

OTI473M515Th216

'Ok, getting somewhere. Brought a bible because I suspected it.'

Jeff mumbles as he rustles its thin pages back and forth, making notes as he does. 'Wow. Someone is very self-righteous. Now, OT stands for Old Testament and I for Isaiah.

'So, the numbers had to mean chapter and verse. Go to Chapter 47, verse 3, and you read: Thy nakedness shall be uncovered, yea, thy shame shall be seen: I will take vengeance, and I will not meet thee as a man.'

'That's so bloody dismissive and angry. He's being accused, demeaned, repudiated and threatened,' I say.

'Agreed,' says Jeff. 'Old Testament bombast in excelsis. The next part is more specific. It's the Book of Micah, Chapter 5, Verse 15. Listen . . .'

'And I will execute vengeance in anger and fury upon the heathen, such as they have not heard.'

Another threat and this one frightens me. Am I being targeted for something Richard did, or is it coincidence that my last name is Heath?

'Don't think it means you. I'd reckon it means Richard was a heathen because he behaved in ways unacceptable to the Biblical morality of the writer.

'The last reference is Thessalonians, 21:6. Seeing it is a righteous thing with God to recompense tribulation to them that trouble you.'

'Suppose that justifies the other quotes and leaving him in my kitchen,' I say, feeling the pain of whoever did this. Jeff ignores me because his forensic mind has galloped on.

'The middle line is Proverbs. pvb1012but . . .

'I reckon it's by a different hand and by the smeared ending it was forced to stop before it had finished.

'Does it say anything different?'

'Hatred stirreth up strifes: but love covereth all sins.'

'Asking for forgiveness?' I suggest.

'Or pleading justification.'

'One more thing,' says Jeff. 'These could have been written by different hands. Perhaps three.'

Isn't that something Trev thought?

Chapter 21

•

October 27th, 1978

Nothing has happened to solve Richard's murder but Trev has reminded us about the over-excited girls at the memorial service, the ones who seemed much too pleased that Richard Metcalfe was dead. From his espresso-duty at Bella's side he's noticed them visiting Richard's parents every Friday. Then they scuttle down Portobello Road to treat themselves at the deli, celebrating something, he's sure.

Trev signals. The girls are coming down the hill and Luciana baits her trap. She puts two handbags onto the shelf beside her. They're Hermes Kelly Bags, a style that has been around for yonks but is now renamed after the actress Grace Kelly refused to give one back after filming To Catch a Thief. Her becoming the reigning Princess of Monaco has enhanced their public image and perceived value.

The girls notice the handbags as they turn into the deli and within milliseconds Luciana has beckoned them over. I don't think they've ever spoken to each other before, but opulence breaks barriers. The girls know what they are looking at. I expect they also know Luciana is a princess with more other titles than any of their family or friends.

'Which one would you like to win?' Luciana lands them with that irresistible question.

'Win? Is there a competition?'

'Not anymore. I'm giving one of these as a raffle prize, raising money for distressed aristocrats. But I thought you'd have an opinion.'

I move closer, pretending to tidy shelves. The girls are silent. I can't tell if this is their usual non-communicative state, or if it's worship of the two handbags or awe at La Principessa's pristine hair and make-up, Chanel suit and grey Tahitian pearls.

Both girls would have been such easy targets for Richard Metcalfe. Each is a middle-class clone, one of thousands of rake-thin teenage girls who wear almost nothing whatever the weather, ditto slop about in flat ballet-style slippers and whose spread fingers are forever shovelling and repacking their long, tangled hair into a greater mess.

Neither is likely to have had an original thought but relies instead on peer groups, films and magazines for everything they think or wear. They're flattered to be asked their opinions about something as special as Kelly bags, one in golden crocodile, the other pimpled black ostrich skin.

'Pick one up. See if one feels better.'

One girl is more outgoing. She grabs the crocodile and threads her skinny left arm through the handles. At once, Luciana is up on her feet.

'That's not the way!'

I've seen this before. Luciana hates the way most women carry a handbag 'these days'. It's why so many blunder through crowds with arms like the splayed legs of a dead chicken, bashing and bruising as they go, if not with their arms, then with their bag.

'D'you see what you are doing wrong?'

Luciana takes back the bag and demonstrates the proper way to hold it. The girls can't understand until she talks them through it step by step. 'D'you see? It's not from the inside but . . . watch this, from the outside.'

She shows the right way once more. She holds the bag flat against her left hip and then slips her left arm through the handle straps from the outside, not from inside, not from the side closer to her body.

Once the girl achieves this, Luciana asks her to walk through the cafe. As she does the quieter one picks up the ostrich and does the same.

Luciana gloats. 'Ecco. Hold it the right way and you see? It stays close to your side when you walk. Do it the other way and your walk kicks it out.' Both girls giggle at the simplicity of their new knowledge.

'So cool,' one of them says. 'And you don't have to spread your arms.'

'It's the way the Queen does it. And any educated woman.'

The advantage is so obvious I wonder why it's not as well-known as the correct way to hold a dinner knife. Except I'd be out of business if I banned everyone who holds their knife like a pen.

Luciana's demonstration of handbag etiquette is followed with silence deepened either by shame at not knowing this simple fact or with complete indifference.

Trev delivers two mugs of mochaccino, our mix of espresso coffee and superior melted chocolate with hot milk that's topped with whipped cream and a caramel sauce he's piped on in a heart shape. It's the most expensive drink we serve and must be what the girls order on their celebratory Fridays.

He puts these onto Luciana's Cheese-Cabin shelf and walks off giving me a wink and a smile. The girls have no chance of getting away. I join Luciana and encourage conversation about handbags and etiquette until Trev brings coffees for Luciana and me, just as we get the girls' names right.

They are Charlie and George, Charlie for Charlotte and George for Georgiana. When Luciana puts the handbags into a holdall on the floor the girls' interest switches off. Their hands swathe through their hair and they look around for something else to divert them.

'You like jewellery?'

Luciana's charm is like a warm bath and the girls soak in it as she pulls out jewel after jewel, encouraging them as they each fondle the pieces, all animal and flower shapes.

'Are these real?' asks George. It's a reasonable question for amateurs to ask but Luciana is not amused. She shoots a glance at me and tightens her lips. I applaud her restraint by smiling back. 'They're real yes, but not signed. On the other hand. . .'

Luciana opens a tumble of jewellers' boxes, red and blue and black velvet, pale holly wood and dyed green shagreen or ray skin. I recognise the names stamped in gold on their satin linings - Cartier, Van Cleef & Arpels, Garrard, Mouawad, Tiffany. These are serious rings, earrings, pendants and brooches, all with enormous stones of transfixing colour.

A spell falls. I'm as hypnotised as Charlie and George by a square-cut pink diamond that splatters sheets of rosy light at us, by a ruby that seems to simmer in blood.

There's something direct and uncompromising about the light and colours the gemstones share with us and I try to think of words to describe them. Noble, are they? Majestic? Mesmerising, for sure.

'What's that blue stuff, then?' Charlie's interest is intense, but her wording is so crass in contrast to the beauty of the pyramid on her finger that it's not deserving of an answer. Yet Luciana explains with patience. 'Sapphire, a rare Kashmir sapphire, only mined for a few years and cut as a sugarloaf cabochon. . .'

'Looks like jelly.'

'Brava! Essatamente.'

Charlie looks up beaming 'Oh was I right?' She giggles. 'I usually get a slap when I say things like that.'

'What month?' George demands.' Y'know, like for birthdays and stuff.'

'As a birthstone? Sapphire is September.'

Whereas Charlie is reverential of the gemstones, George is excited by them. She's jigging with excitement.

'Cool! Hey babe - you should get one of them things now you're getting your money back. Like yeah, it would've been the baby's birthstone.'

Charlie leaps to her feet, spilling her sticky drink

over the jewellery. She backhands George's face, and then tucks her elbows in and pummels her by flailing her forearms and open hands.

Luciana jumps to avoid brown liquid and whipped cream on her navy-piped, pink Chanel suit but this knocks her coffee onto Charlie and George.

The true mental age of the teenagers becomes apparent. Both girls stand incapable of coping or voicing their feelings. They utter meaningless yelps, the sort of noise other post-pubescents might understand but that have no purchase with adults. Between these, brushing mochaccino off themselves and pushing their hair back with the same sticky hands, their minds are occupied.

Trev fusses in, horrified as ever at anything messy. He dumps paper napkins on the shelf to inhibit the flood of mochaccino and shoves handsful of paper napkins at the rest of us. He opens the door to my flat and I push Luciana and the girls up the stairs, mopping up drips and spots as we go.

Trev yells up that the bags haven't been splashed and that he'll dry and guard the jewellery.

George turns to push past me and run from the deli. I can't tell if she is crying or laughing.

Perhaps it's both.

Chapter 22

Upstairs Luciana comforts Charlie. She's calm as she soaks, sponges and wipes using cold water and my tea towels, concentrating on the girl's stains and not her own. Her kindness is not an act by Luciana, yet there's something in her eyes that tells me she hasn't forgotten why we want to talk to the girl called Charlie. The matter of Richard Metcalfe's murder.

Luciana's belief in gemstones' ability to pull people out of their usual world has worked better than I expected. We now have Charlie alone and dependent.

'What was that about a baby?' Luciana asks, raising her hand for another cloth from me. Charlie sniffles.

'Did your Mum know?'

Charlie holds her breath for five seconds and then flings her arms around Luciana and sobs into her shoulder. I'm betting her mouthy friend Georgiana was the only other person who knew.

I have to turn away. I run water fast and fill up the filter jug so I can make tea.

'She'd kill me,' Charlie sobs.

Several tissues later she straightens her back.

'It was him, wasn't it? That Richard. He didn't well, you know, do anything about condoms or anything.'

'You could have said no,' Luciana says, being insensitive, I think. Charlie doesn't care. 'You can't say no, not to him. I couldn't . . . no one could.'

The look she shoots at me seems a plea for complicity. What did that beast-boy tell her about me and him? I'll kill him, I hear myself think. Well, you do say that, don't you?

'So, you didn't have the baby?' Luciana asks.

'Richard paid to, you know, somewhere private, thousands he said, so it was safe... Then afterwards, just when I thought it was all over, he wants me to pay him back. If I don't, he's telling Mummy everything, even about me and George and everything.'

I feel as furious as she does. I flush with her pain and anger, sharing her flashbacks of horror and betrayal. I chant to myself, making a refrain of 'relax, relax, relax, you are relaxed and confident'.

No. It doesn't work. There's too much else going on.

Now I understand why Charlie was laughing at Richard's memorial. She must have thought her misery was over and her secret safe.

It would have been, if Luciana's plan to loosen tongues with the liberating light of gemstones hadn't worked on George.

I'm not sure I should hear any more, or I'll be a weeping wreck. There's nothing dainty about the raw feelings of a teenage girl who has terminated an underage pregnancy and then been blackmailed by the very person who caused the problem. My senses are picking up all of Charlie's distress and it's not comfortable. I feel her rage and hate at Richard's duplicity but I'm an adult man, not a damaged teenage girl. I suck back a few of my more determined sobs and brush my eyes.

The sooner this is over the better for us all.

'What about Richard's parents, the Metcalfes,' I

ask. 'Did they know?'

'I didn't want them to know but George told them. After Richard died, and, well, it was awful for them.'

I hear an alarm. She's naive enough to feel sorry for the Metcalfes and then switch the blame to herself. Just as Belinda seemed to sympathise with the murderer or murderers. She musn't go down that route. I settle enough to ask about the Friday visits in a calm voice.

'George fixed it. She wanted to make sure I wouldn't have to pay anymore. You know, in case it was them rather than Richard who wanted me to pay back the money.'

'Was it?'

'No. But George made them pay back what Richard had already taken from me.'

'How did they react?'

'Angry.'

'At what?'

'Everything.'

'Like?'

'Everything.

She wants to be prompted. Luciana and I don't want to guide her in anyway. We win.

'Well, everything. That Richard hadn't told them. About the abortion. That he was making me repay money that he didn't even need. That they'd lost a grandchild . . .'

Luciana stirs. I put a hand on her shoulder and she understands she should stay quiet.

Uncertain she's doing the right thing, but anxious

to please us, Charlie continues. 'Nothing, that's what they kept saying. Nothing, over and over. They said Richard hadn't left them with nothing in return for all they had given him.'

Ah yes. What went around didn't come around. Shouldn't have been a surprise but it is to most people and what an extra burden for the Metcalfes to bear.

It's a struggle not to identify with all I imagine the Metcalfes are suffering. I turn back and speak over my shoulder.

'Why go every week? Couldn't they just give you a lump sum?'

'They said they didn't want to do anything out of the ordinary. Because Portobello is using everything to blacken Richard's memory. She tells people we go there because we are the kindest girls on Portobello for taking the time to visit them when no-one else wants to know them. That's what people are supposed to believe, anyway . . .'

'So what? You sit and talk. She makes tea? What?'

'She opens the door and takes us upstairs to get the money. It's in an envelope on the desk with all those cuttings from newspapers and stuff.'

'What do they say?'

'Nothing. It's horrible. He sits there crying and she holds his hand and sprays stuff into the air. It's like someone's killed them but they're still alive. Like zombies and stuff. I told George she shouldn't have told them . . . It would have all been over.'

'You don't want the money back?'

'I don't need it, no. It's different for lots of the others.'

'Others. What? Who?'

'Others he was taking money from. He thought it was funny. Called it a Secrets Tax. Said it was teaching Portobello that anything that like feels nice or looks nice or tastes nice has got a price and that the sooner that's learned the better.'

So, Richard Metcalfe was as mad and avaricious as he was beautiful. With a twisted Messianic mission to teach the world to be suspicious of people like himself.

Luciana and I are silent, working this through our thoughts.

'He didn't do so much sex because he fancied so many people,' Charlie adds. 'Or even liked sex that much. He did sex so you would pay him to shut up about having it with him.'

'Where did you get the money from to pay Richard? It must have been quite a lot every week.' Luciana's question gets a shrug from Charlie. 'My parents are rich. They give me heaps. And I know where they hide stuff around the house. It's just hard to get a big lot at once. I spend it too fast.'

'So, paying was never the problem?'

'No way! It was people knowing. Like my Mum and Dad. Then I wouldn't have any money or be allowed out or . . .'

In a flash her focus changes. 'Is George downstairs? She will be, won't she?'

No wonder Richard targeted her. A born victim, comfortable always in the arms of discomfort. Still, that's no excuse for him to have blackmailed her over an aborted baby, his baby.

'After the memorial, I remember thinking everything would be over. That's why I couldn't see why I was being threatened now Richard was dead everything should be over.'

'Still being threatened? Who?'

Charlie blanches and sways. 'Don't! I can't. It would get worse.'

It's not over. Richard' blackmailing is continuing but by whom? How many others in Portobello are anxious that if I find Richard's murderer I'll also discover why they have been paying his Secrets Tax?

I can't think about this without my heart fluttering and my mood darkening. My sympathy for the Metcalfes is dissolving yet their intimate grief for a lost grandchild determines me to work harder to find their son's murderer.

Later Luciana and I noted again there'd been not an iota of sympathy for the aborted baby. We wonder if Charlie's attitude to human mortality might extend to doing a bit of killing herself, revenging herself by murdering Richard. But she is too thin and weak to make any of the wounds we've seen or to carry his body into the shop's kitchen. Of course, she might have had George's help, but we agree George would have told someone by now.

Except, they have a greater secret to keep.

Of course, that's what Charlie meant by 'even me and George and everything' and this is an explanation for Charlie being so anxious to make up with

George, even though she'd been both bullied and abandoned by her.

Luciana has talked about this. Many a man is so threatened by lesbianism that he rapes, believing this to be a practical therapy. Was Richard Metcalfe so arrogant that he believed he could change Charlie's orientation? We decide he was and forced Charlie to come face to face with her physical self by becoming pregnant. That explains not using condoms, which he must have used in every other circumstance.

But it doesn't explain who killed him.

Charlie's story has also suggested a new motive for Richard's murder. What if Charlie's parents had found out about the baby and wanted to kill him? What if other victims were just as fed up or frightened by what he might tell someone?

What else might Richard Metcalfe have done to make someone hit him so hard, to move his body and then plan something unspeakable in my kitchen? The answer? He could have done whatever the worst recesses of your mind can imagine. I'll believe anything about that boy. He's Portobello Road's Dorian Gray. Except his hideous portrait was suppurating inside him.

In a single hour of a single Friday afternoon we've followed up an important lead but also dismissed any idea that Charlie and George are blackmailers or are the murderers. Even so, the afternoon raises more questions than it solves. Nastier questions than I ever imagined.

I'm in bed but the slightest noise wakes me. What

if I should have heeded the warnings? What if there were multi-perpetrators in my kitchen, just as there was in Agatha Christie's Murder on the Orient Express?

How many of Richard's other victims might be out there planning to victimise me for my investigations? Where and when? Will I know, get enough warning, be able to defend myself?

I'm frightened. As the hours pass I drift in and out of a sort of nervy stupor until another image of being pursued startles me into full consciousness. The sole way I'll get any real sleep is to face up to the problem and decide what to do about it.

I sit up without turning the light on. The way to solve this problem is not to give in to threats but to discover the basis for the threats.

It takes a while, but I remember something Princess Luciana and I agreed on months ago. No matter how tough or threatening things got it would be wrong to let a murderer get away with what had been done.

Not sure I should tell you this but where some people might pray for guidance, I try to work out what Batman would have done. He wouldn't doubt a quest. Neither must I.

Like all Super-Heroes, my mission is to do good and to defeat evil doers. It's sad, I know, but emulating the morality of my comic-book heroes gives me confidence.

I give a little snort of laughter at myself. But it's not that much different from praying, is it?

The thought does little to help sleep.

Chapter 23

Luciana has pointed out a shop-floor romance she has watched for the last months. Mary is a shy Australian girl who puts that aside when serving, and customers love her attentive personality.

One of the deli's newer customers is attracted to her and she's reciprocating, even though he is twice her age, say mid-30s. Tall, dark and with striking charisma, he's welcomed in the deli as relief from the usual dour customer at this dreary time of the year.

His name is Orlando Something Hyphenated and there's every sign he has good Establishment background, something heard in accent, seen in clothes, manners and general bearing. Always wears very good shoes with leather soles.

'So reassuring,' Luciana observes but adds, 'Except he walks with his knees out. A true gentleman doesn't do that. It's a sure sign of weak self-confidence.'

I agree. I reckon Orlando tries too hard, is too well dressed, as though he doesn't have the confidence to be casual. When I suggested this to Luciana, she screwed up her face. I took it as a sign she agrees but doesn't want to be seen to do so.

I've watched Orlando and Mary together in Gabriel's wine bar and she was sparkling in a way she never shows when not serving. Some on the deli floor suspect ill motives of romances with an age difference but I've seen plenty work around here. Not just straight couples but male and female gay pairs, too. Is this because those who aren't mainstream feel more comfortable in Notting Hill and migrate here in greater numbers? It makes Portobello life more colourful and as food seems important to these relationships they add life to the deli, too.

This evening Orlando comes into the deli quite late and Mary isn't working. It seems an opportunity to take a paternal interest in Mary's future. That's what Luciana and Jeremy seem to expect from me.

'It's Orlando, isn't? Friend of Luciana?' I say, intercepting him.

'It is. The princess and I have been friends for ages.' I click that Luciana's title is perhaps more important than she might be.

'Can I help you find something?'

'I'm looking for snacks, something for Mary and me before we are out to the Albert Hall. We'll eat later, but . . .'

'Bread or crackers?'

'Nothing heavy, crackers I suppose. But filling . . .'

'Got anything at home?'

'Some pears. . . any use?'

'Good start.'

I cut Orlando a wedge of Farmhouse Brie, as soft as butter and without a whiff of ammonia. Brie with pear is one of those culinary combinations where one and one make three on the palate – and more. Then I offer a few slices of Parma ham, not the best but the most available of Italy's air-dried prosciuttos. Pear is much better than melon with air-dried hams.

'Do you know my smoked salmon pate?'

'Heard about it from Mary.'

'And she likes it?'

'Raves.'

I fill a small pot and say it is with my compliments. While he is off guard at the generosity (it's quite expensive) I make the plunge. 'Luciana says you have something to do with music, singing is it?'

'Not me. I'm an agent for those who do. I sell others' talent, not my own.'

'A talent of its own, I'd think.'

'Ha ha, thank you. Mary and I are off to hear a soprano I'm interested in representing.'

'Better not keep you then. Hope it goes well.'

I'm not sure what to think. Except that suspicion someone is wearing a social mask is often justified in and around Portobello Road.

By now we've put up bright decorations and snowflake lights to add twinkle to our seasonal specialties, many made by locals, even the almond-paste stuffed Stollen loaves.

Did you know a Stollen represents the swaddled baby Jesus as laid in the manger of the Bethlehem stable? I've learned not to tell this to children. Biting into samples of a sleeping baby upsets some more than conscience and ears can bear.

Next morning is Saturday and I'm desperate to dig around in the Victory Antique Arcade, almost opposite the deli. Trev wants to know what Meredith is doing as she dashes in and out of the arcade.

'Something's going on there with the boys, too,' he suggests.

'Boys?'

'Yeah. Always running in and out with bags of stuff. Different ones. But doing the same things.'

I've learned not to ignore Trev's instincts, but this is not the time to explore. By 9.30 four boys and a girl have been caught stealing from our Christmas displays. Nothing expensive. Chocolates, shortbread, miniature pannetone. That sort of thing. Trev reckons some of them are those who dart in and out of The Victory Arcade.

Each one is cheeky, smart-arsed and bare-faced about it, mocking who ever catches them. They know it's a waste of time for us to call the police.

They can't be charged if they're under 10, because the law says they don't understand criminal culpability. What a joke. They've been taught thievery with their mother's milk. Their families expect them to make a pretty profit from picking pockets and outright theft every Saturday. In their circles pregnancy is not another mouth to feed but welcomed as another mouth to feed you.

Stealing on a busy Saturday by kids who can't be charged is a brazen and annoying way to interfere with the deli, but this seems worse than usual. I sense it's a continuing follow up to the threats made in Ladbroke Grove after Richard's memorial service. They've waited until we are busiest, just when it will hurt most. If a deli doesn't make huge sales and profits in the weeks up to Christmas it may as well not open again. The dilution of staff time while they cope with the thieves means a loss of sales to genuine customers.

Of all days, I'm committed to seeing Mrs Cheesecake. She lives close to where Rillington Place used to be, infamous for the terrace house where John Christie had sex with dead women he'd gassed before nailing them up behind his kitchen wall. Necrophilia? Is that the name for it? How did he live with the smell of those rotting bodies? Demolition, reconfiguration of streets and rebuilding has obliterated Rillington Place, making pointless pickings for ghouls.

Mrs Cheesecake has sent a lawyer's letter demanding I watch her bake an orange cheesecake to my recipe or she's going to sue me. When I stopped buying from her, others did too and she blames me for loss of reputation and income, swearing she followed my recipe and that I must have sabotaged her with an inferior version.

She's typical of a stratum of Notting Hill/Portobello single women. They're asset-rich in an expensive flat or mews house or house, but which has been earned through divorce or separation rather than personal exertion or talent.

They are fierce about the jobs they take on to ensure independence yet scream inside for someone else to win the bread, to pedestal them as the special, pampered woman they believe they deserve to be. They flirt as much as any dirty-minded teenager.

Mrs Cheesecake is belligerent the moment she opens the door. 'I've started already.' I smile, suggesting I'm pleased. 'Neither of us has all the time in the world.' I'm impressed at how warm and sympathetic I sound.

She leads me down to the basement, a knocked through room with a few steps up to an unkempt back garden.

What I see is a market stall with superior cooking facilities. Apart from the cooker and a metal prep table, every surface heaves with 'stuff' I often hear defended as 'collections' and 'heritage memories'. Open-lidded biscuit tins glitter with tumbled costume jewellery. Fading theatre programmes slither about in a couple of weathered trugs. There are shadow puppets hanging from the ceiling, seashells on the floor and teddy bears arranged to simulate copulation in one of two old rocking chairs.

My nose tells me every page, head, bead, box and can is impregnated with cooking vapours and that each has harvested fat, dust and dirt, perhaps for years. Is this what masked the flavour in her version of my orange cheesecakes?

Mrs Cheesecake affects a cook's white tunic, fastened with two rows of blackcurrant-like buttons. It looks professional but means nothing and I soon see why she failed. She's impatient.

The melted butter is too hot when she adds it to the curd cheese, cream and egg mixture, losing lightness that will never be recovered. She also uses artificial orange-flower water that costs twice as much as the real thing from Lebanon yet tastes half as good as that genuine distillation of bitter-orange blossoms.

Despite out-dated, oversized butterfly frames she misreads the recommended portion and uses less than I would. It's going to make little difference to the cooked cheesecake, but already I can't be bothered pointing this out.

So far there's no reason for Mrs Cheesecake's product to taste so very different from mine. I want to be back in the shop but bite my tongue, until I see her grating orange skin on to her wooden chopping board.

The vital flavour in orange zest is in the oil, the fine spray from grating you see when the light's right. Grating zest onto wood rather than over the cheesecake mixture means most is absorbed by the board. That's why there was no profound orange flavour in her cheesecake. It's such a common mistake, explaining tasteless lemon meringue and Key lime tarts. A certificate on the wall shows she graduated from a well-known culinary school. Don't they know the zest/wooden board thing?

I point this failing out with discretion. For a few seconds she seems grateful. Then she turns and slams the grater onto the inevitable pine sideboard behind her and a green-crazed serving dish falls to the floor. It has held an untidy stack of papers and photographs. As these tumble to the floor, I reach to grab one.

It's a Polaroid taken in this kitchen of Richard Metcalfe naked, showing off his bum and grinning over his shoulder. His brutal, piercing eyes tell a colder story.

'That bloody boy!'

She screams, snatching at the print. Her hoarse anger batters the pots and pans hanging from the ceiling and bounces back louder. I wince, but this encourages her. She turns any insult into a positive sign of interest in her.

Her voice drops. 'Everything's gone wrong since . . .' When she sees my disinterest, she stops and snatches again. I let her have the photograph. She rips it into shreds but keeps these in her hands.

'He was blackmailing you?' I ask.

She interprets even this as flattery, and simpers. 'Not in a big way. Not money, anyway.' She titters, pretending it was unimportant but flings her hands around as she speaks and then folds her arms hard against her chest.

Blackmail is blackmail and it has hurt.

'Just cakes and things, presents he gave away to make him look like Mr Big. To help him seduce other sad old women like me.'

I know she wants me to protest that she's neither sad nor old. I won't. I've not the time for therapy, not on a Saturday. The deli will be heaving. Even more, I need to investigate what Trev thinks is suspicious about the gloomy stalls of the Victory Antiques Arcade.

'Why didn't you refuse, say something to someone,' I demand, knowing there's impatience in my voice.

'He was half my age! Less, in fact, the same sort of age as my sons. This place belongs to my ex-husband's family. The boys are at boarding school, paid for by them. They'd turn me out as being unfit. I'd have nowhere if they knew.'

'And so you killed him.'

I'm joking but sometimes the most obvious solution is the truth but the hardest to find. She'd has the temperament to do it.

'I thought about it!' she says, laughing. 'No, I just wanted a little company.'

'And he was willing to give it, in return for . . .'

'Ha! You can talk. He had you, too, didn't he? I bet that's cost you a pretty penny! I can imagine what he made you do so he could bring me goodies.'

I see. Richard Metcalfe stole from me to reward his victims before then taking money from them. That made me an exception. I paid for something I did not get. He didn't have me but there's little use protesting.

I thought it didn't matter that I was helping the shop's income by turning a blind eye to his stealing, but Mrs Cheesecake has revealed he made me complicit in his dirty dealings.

Her eyes glitter as she senses a victory. She unfolds her arms, reaches into a drawer for a cigarette and lights this by bending to the gas hob.

Smoking in a kitchen is worse than making a tasteless orange cheesecake.

'Here's the deal. You drop that lawyer's letter business and never repeat that lie about Richard and me. I'll not tell the council about you smoking in the domestic kitchen where you cater professionally.'

Her sudden, child-like voice wheedles and she looks sideways with assumed coyness. An index finger taps her lower lip. 'I'm making very good Christmas Mince Tarts this year.'

The belief in her persuasive power is tragic. I know she's boiling with shame and with rage inside, yet she wants a triumph, any sort of success and at any price.

'So are we,' I say with a smile that's as light and natural as hers attempts to be. The difference is that my smile will last after her door is closed.

When I turn into Portobello Road from Colville Terrace, I see there's a knot of policemen outside the deli. I run and push against the downstream surge of browsing foreigners. They're so togged up against the cold they don't notice my elbows.

Sharp young voices slice through the market's multi-lingual babble, protesting about 'brutality'. I slow to a walk. The little bastards are not going to know I am rattled. Stay cool, I say to myself. Stay cool. Relax, relax.

'Yoo-hoo! I want to tell you something!' Long John Silver waves an arm high over the crowd. He grabs and stops me and bends to my ear.

Chapter 24

'It's probably not important but you never know.' Milky coffee and Gauloise cigarettes flood his breath. I hold mine.

'It wasn't just his sex life she screamed about. Rubbish. It was the bags of rubbish left in their doorway. She blamed him, said it was people paying Richard back, telling him what they thought of him. She screamed at him to get rid of them as soon as she found one.'

'Did he?'

'Wheeled them away like a good boy. Now she has to do it but I don't see so many, well, now he's gone.'

Long John has seen my eyes darting from him to the shop. He looks over his shoulder. 'Better let you go. Something's not right there. Police an' all . . .'

There have been scuffles. Jeremy, Luciana and Trev have been fed up and got tough with the young shoplifters, manhandling them from the deli by their collars and sleeves. Long John Silver points out that their wails have attracted faces I know. Man in Black and Barry the ex-Sports teacher. It's their rough intervention that led to fisticuffs.

There's a stand-off. I can see that although Jeremy, Trev and Luciana welcome the police, those other two blokes are anxious to be off. Me, I'd like to know how those two got there so fast and where they might go, because now I had my first solid evidence that they are associated with the organised nicking from my shelves.

What's their game? It must be more than wanting me to forget finding who duffed up Richard Metcalfe.

I realise they will have antennas out for the rest of the day and resign myself to a day on the floor of greetings and taking money.

They might claim a victory today. I'll have the Victory Antiques Arcade another time.

. . .

Luciana and I are having a quiet moment together, late in the afternoon when the deli is quiet. She's telling me about the first night of 'L'Africaine' at the Royal Opera House a few weeks ago and is raving about the young Argentinian tenor Placido Domingo, who sings Vasco da Gama, the other name for the opera.

When a Portobello visitor stops and claps his hand to his face exclaiming, 'Paradise', Luciana jumps up.

'O Paradiso!' she shouts and getting no response from me adds, 'It's the opera's greatest aria and Domingo brought down the house, but I was distracted by the woman sitting in front of me. Gorgeous embroidered gown, proper first night standard, but when she wriggled to drop her stole from her shoulders. . .'

She stops and wrinkles her eyes. 'A mink cross that was white with cloudy black borders. Is it called Koh-i-Noor? Ma, non importante!

'My point is the label of the dress was sticking up, held there by her necklace. Ruined the moment for me.'

'Because?'

'Because it can't have been haute couture. High Street, I expect.'

'Don't haute couture frocks have labels?'

'They do but they are sewn flat into the lining.'

'What's your point, Luciana?'

'How did Belinda know Richard's red dress was a Rahvis?'

'Ah, I remember. She said that's what was on the label.'

'Al punto!'

'So, she'd seen the label and it must have been there when Richard left.'

'Exactamente! but remember the photographs. There was no label on the dress Richard was wearing on your table.'

I run upstairs and bring some prints down.

'Aspetto! Look! The lining has been pulled up at the neckline. See the shape there? The label's been cut out. And not with much care.'

'When?' Trev interrupts. 'If we know that, we might know who did what to Richard.' He has been earwigging and he's right. But what do we do next? How do we find out what has happened to the label?

Did whoever cut it out keep it as a souvenir?

'And where's them high heels what he was supposed to be wearing?'

Why haven't Luciana and I asked that before?

Chapter 25

There's a new wine bar on the corner of Kensington Park Road and Westbourne Grove. It's a wood-lined dungeon in my eyes but this growing trend of wine bars is a welcome step up from a pub's sickening smell of slopped beer, of overweight men and over-made-up women. I know that's an extreme view, but that's my experience of such of Portobello's frosted-window pubs as the Duke of Wellington, the one closest to the deli. The local shout is that it's the headquarters of local crims, but how would anyone know when you can't see in or out of it?

Wine bars attract more attractive people and are quieter, too, great for overhearing what is best kept quiet. Even better when a few glasses have been downed. Yet, it doesn't matter what you drink or where, your hair and clothes still emerge stinking of cigarette smoke.

The wine-bar's ebullient young host Gabriel is French Canadian and fancies me. He shows it by always offering a glass of champagne. I dare not to think what it might be, but it tastes good and it's free.

I've had to escape the deli and crystallise all that's been thrown at me. The whereabout of the gold shoes and the label, the Man in Black and, well you know . . . heaps of stuff.

There are few drinkers here so early after reopening time and most are young, another appeal of this wine bar trend. A noisy group in the furthest, fuggiest, darkest corner includes Charlie and George, who nod but then turn to face into the group.

'Regulars?' I ask.

'Very, and always intense.'

'About?'

'Hard to say but I hear Richard's name a lot. You know, the one in the . . . '

'Wearing a red dress, I do know. What about him?'

'Favourite place, this. It was like watching a horror movie, the way he would work a group and then concentrate on just one.'

'Which made her feel special in front of her friends.

'Or him. He didn't care that one.'

'You?

'Thought about it but I didn't fancy him being anywhere near the cash register or me.'

'Sticky fingers?'

'And the rest, my dear.'

I sink the rest of the fizzy stuff and order a glass of Muscadet, Notting Hill's current craze, putting money on the bar as I do, not wanting further obligation to Gabriel.

'Know what they talk about most?'

'Hard to say but there's definitely a secret and definitely a disagreement about keeping it or not.'

'They been here long?'

'Since opening.

'Drunk much?'

'Sucking it down.'

'Give me a bottle of what they most like – no, there's four of them. Give me two. Let's loosen things.'

There's surprise when I push the bottles into the jumble of glasses and ashtrays on the table.

'This is to say thank you, Charlie and George, thanks for your help. You were real cool, as you'd say.'

A handsome dark-haired youth affects nonchalance. I know him from the deli as Nigel Double-Barrelled and there's suspicion and fear in his voice that he's trying to disguise as mockery.

'What? Helped in the shop? Not them working there, surely? Not groovy!' His high giggle embarrasses him and is choked back by sucking on his cigarillo.

'Nothing like that. They helped me understand Richard Metcalfe better, how he worked and well, how he lived. You know, financially . . .'

There's no need to dob in Charlie. Flickering eyes, deep sucks on cigarettes and nervy swallows of wine confirm this is shared knowledge. I walk away, hoping the free wine will loosen them up. I ignore them for 25 minutes until I hear the noise level has risen and then amble back.

'I don't suppose any of you know where the party was that Richard last went to? He wore a red dress and high-heeled golden shoes. That's all we know, except that's the last time anyone saw him in Portobello Rd.'

Nothing is coming back to me, but the group is fiddling and nervous, so I press on. 'Must have been close to here because he walked from Portobello. In the dress and heels. Any of you live that close?'

'All of us,' says Charlie, sounding frightened. Dark looks threaten her, but she's defended by Rupert, known as Red.

'She's right, isn't she? We all do!'

I pull out paper on which I have written the address found on Richard's bedroom mirror.

'Is this one of them?'

Rupert crushes out a cigarette and there's silence while he fills everyone's glass, spilling as he does. He throws down his wine and swings his thick red hair so it cascades down the back of his gold-frogged military jacket. Slamming his emptied glass on the table he shouts, 'I'm sick of this.'

'Of what, Red?' I ask, moving close.

'Of everyone knowing but no-one telling.'

He grabs someone else's glass, empties that and slumps.

'Alright. End of the shit. No-one murdered Richard. He fell off those stupid heels. Fell downstairs in a great arc and landed with his head on a brass planter. There. And, no, I don't know why we've kept it a secret.'

Only Jem looks relieved.

'Are we in trouble? asks George, defensive and aggressive as ever.

'With the police, you mean? Not necessarily,' I add, hoping the extra wine and screwed down discomfort will dislodge more truths. 'Depends on how you explain putting him under my deli and then planning something with a knife and sausage maker.'

'On my honour, Sir, 'Nigel protests, 'all our honour. We know nothing about that. Too freaky, man. It wasn't us and anyway the fall didn't kill him . . .'

'Yeah, what would we know about how a freaking sausage machine works?' demands George. The privileged nodding heads barricade themselves in class-based ignorance, thinking this is defence enough.

My best ploy is to shut them down. That often forces someone to have a last, revealing word.

'OK. We'll agree it was an accident. So, there's no need to involve police. Not if you are telling the truth about the fall not killing him . . .'

George puts up a finger as her mouth twitches. I hold up a forbidding palm. The longer I silence her now, the more she'll say later. It's like ignoring the first whistle of a boiling kettle.

'Come and see me in the shop, Rupert. Soon. Bring any of the others you want.'

I leave the wine bar with a big new question.

If Richard didn't die after the fall, what happened next?

How did he get into a gardening bag?

When was Richard slashed and murdered. And by whom?

My possible answers shock me.

Yet even they don't explain why I should find him laid out in my kitchen.

Chapter 26

●

'I watched them all the time, so I'll tells you why.'

Trev has made an interesting observation about the deep friendship between Jem and his friend, the still missing Freddy. Even though Jem went to a private school, he and Freddy were inseparable out of school hours.

'They was the same, innit?' Trev continues, his eyes not leaving the shelves where he is twisting and straightening flat cans.

'You mean, weren't they?'

'Sorry, Boss. Forgot about the innits.'

I wait. Trev is getting his mind as organised as the Portuguese sardines in olive oil that were being given their regular turn to keep the oil penetration even.

'Well, you know how Freddy was mixed, and so didn't look white? Jem's the same. His father ain't white neither. The name tells you.'

Obvious! Jem's always-absent father Professor Lopez is either Spanish, or Mexican or a mix of both. Both boys looked different from others but liked one another because of their dark eyes and rich skin colour.

'Must have been nice for them, I reckon,' says Trev. 'Yeah, and I bet Jem's mum was happy for his father always to be in the States. Perhaps it was her idea, y'know, so no-one said nothing about mixed marriages.'

'Mixed? Spanish or Mexican and white American?

'This ain't groovy King's Road.'

Yet again Meredith has become part of the story. But did I want to talk to her yet? No, I decided, but I need to know much more about her boy's friendship with Freddy.

Meredith had been in the shop earlier, leaving an order for us to make up for collection later. Freddy's mother Lena should be at her house and might let me in.

She is and she does but she's nervous, biting her thin lips and checking every hair is clipped inside her charlady headscarf. She isn't sure when Meredith might return, so I ask straight out if I can see Jem's bedroom.

It is packed with sporting paraphernalia and schoolbooks, discarded clothing and dismantled scientific instruments. A telescope on a tripod dominates. I take Polaroid pictures to share with Luciana and Trev. No way I would risk an ordinary camera and having developers ruin them.

Two special things strike me. Against one wall there are bunk beds and I presume this is an American thing. That's where Freddy would have slept when he stayed over but there's no sign of him. And there is a unique ceiling.

The bedroom's roof is a dark blue, very dark, like space, I suppose. It's textured with hundreds of small, hand painted silver stars, and a few are emphasised with something reflective. When I stand on a chair, I see these are fragments, broken or crushed, of mirror and glass set micro-mosaic-like in a glue of some sort. Under the biggest I just make out a tiny photograph, a baby's face, an angel I suppose. Sentimental for a teenage boy, I think, and wonder what Trev has to say about that.

Lena has rethought letting me in. I hide the camera and prints and sit as though thinking hard. It's the truth. I've reminded myself about knowing everything about a victim before I know anything about the perpetrator. By the time Lena opens the bedroom door I know I must see her house and Freddy's bedroom.

The block on the estate where Lena lives is on the north side of Westbourne Grove. The brick building is low and dull. There's no lift and she sighs an apology for that, her surroundings and for the interior of her apartment. It's no surprise Lena is happy to spend so much time at Meredith's and other classier homes.

Now she's living alone, her domestic values have slipped and I wonder again how anyone bothers to keep their place clean and tidy when they are paid to keep others like that. Where is the incentive?

Photos of Freddy are everywhere. In his room at least I see her anguish has been focussed into what she knows best. The bedroom is spotless and polished and perfect but there's no sense of life or love. To Lena, life must mean order and that's how she shows love. Trev should've been her son, not Freddy.

Lena points out books on space and on astronomy. A separate pile is magazines and books about predictions based on the stars by a constellation of minor personalities.

'Freddy loved that drivel about astrology. Could tell you anything about anyone if he knew their birthday.'

'Is that something he shared with Jem?'

'Them two! They'd stay up all night if it was clear. Lugging that telescope thing with them.'

'He must have loved Jem's star ceiling.'

'They done that together. But they was very secret about it.'

'Something to do with an angel?'

Lena throws up her arms to indicate she hadn't been party to the secret. The saggy sleeve of her knitted cardigan jumbles the top of a chest of drawers and she turns to tidy it. I had seen something L-shaped and ask about it.

'One of them new inhalers things. Helped him breathe.'

'Did Freddy have asthma?'

'No, just a type of allergy that affected his breathing.'

She purses her lips with anger. 'Them Jamaican boys downstairs and them damned smoking that marie-juana!'

'They made Freddy smoke pot?'

'Call it what you like! He knew he'd get a good beating from me if he did . . .'

'So, what?'

'That stinky smoke. Up and down the stair well and even insides here when the windows or door was open. The stronger the smell, the harder it was for

Freddy to breathe. He developed what them quacks called super-sensitivity or something. Those spray things are a life saver. Most of the time.'

'Most?'

'Well, who knows what's done him in? It was getting worse that pot-smoke thing, but you couldn't stop the boys smoking so we was trying to move. That's why he was always out in the open air but even that was dangerous for him, especially at Carnival time. I reckon that's what's happened. He was caught out. Some of the buggers would mock him and knock the inhaler from him. Blow smoke at him and laugh when he gasped and staggered. I seen them do that on the stairs here. That's what might have happened and then . . .'

'You told that to the police?' Lena shrugged and rolled her eyes.

'It must have been a problem at Jem's place, too.'

'He didn't go much, not anymore. That Mrs Lopez! She was always smoking and having people smoke there. Jem hates her for it because Freddy wasn't safe there.'

'But he did go.'

'Not often. Stayed less and less. Mainly in summer, when all the windows could be open.'

'Like August, during Carnival?'

The mention of Carnival, when Freddy went missing, distresses her.

'So, Freddy was with Jem for Carnival?'

'Who else? But Jem'd said it wasn't a good idea to stay over. He'd come back home, Freddy told me.'

'When did Jem last see him?'

'He says he waved him goodbye late Monday night, the big night.'

'Believe him?'

Lena nods. I feel we have switched to sympathy for how Jem must feel, knowing now that he was saying goodbye to Freddy forever.

'He was my life, everything . . .'

'His father?'

Lena looks at me without wavering for a long time, then sighs and sinks her head. 'Around but not around.'

'You're divorced, separated?'

'Never married, was I?'

Lena lifts her head. There's challenge in her eyes. She looks as though she expects me to dismiss what she is going to say.

'It was rape, weren't it? In one of them sheds in the mews where the stallholders' fruit and veg gets stored overnight. I still hates the smell of oranges.'

'Report him?'

'Told me I wouldn't live if I did. I believed him. Even though he was black, the police would've taken his side, not me.'

'Because?'

'Well, I was, well, the rozzers knew I was keen on the black boys. Been caught a couple of times in them sheds. And I fancied him, didn't I? I'd told me mates about him.'

'So, something go wrong?'

'Didn't want to wear a rubber, did he? When I said

no, he went bananas – not what I should say I suppose.'

'Must have been hard to have a kid like that yourself.'

'What can you do? I didn't have no money to get rid of it and, well, I liked the idea of having someone to myself. Didn't want his father to have anything to do with Freddy.

'But he knew him, his father did. He works on one of them trucks what collects the rubbish from the fruit and veg market every day.

'He knew about Freddy, but Freddy never knew who he was. That right?'

'Right. But he knows what's happened. He come around, I'll give him that. But I sent him packing quick smart. It's Freddy what needed him, not me.'

'You sure about that?' I ask.

'He said that, too!' Lena says, primping in a mirror as she does. 'Cheeky bugger! He never married neither, you know.'

'What's his name, Lena, Freddy's father?'

Her eyes meet mine again but are then lidded. As she struggles to speak, tears like tropical rain flop to the floor, landing like the regular, soft tick of a clock in another room.

'I'd loved him, y'know. I would have married him, even after what he, what happened.'

Lena wipes her eyes with a swift swipe of the back of her hand and sits up very straight, proud of what she's revealing.

'Frederick. That's his name. Not Freddy, Frederick.'

Chapter 27

It's not long before I see Rupert the Red again. He's shuffling outside the deli, with Nigel Double-Barrelled, Charlie and George huddled behind him. I'm checking the Stiltons, ensuring we have enough perfect whole cheeses for Christmas. Each is about 16lbs weight, and I manage their ripeness by channelling into them with a hollow cheese iron that pulls out a long tubular sample. According to what I find, the cheeses are moved into or out of the deli's warmth or the chilled air of the Cheese Cabin, which is where they are held once I judge them as good as I can get.

This visit is more important, so I drop everything, rushing upstairs ahead of them to ensure there are no images of Richard around. Then I wonder if it would have speeded things up if there were.

The four don't speak and spread between the bean bag and chesterfield. None of them wants a drink. After silent urging by the others, Rupert the Red stands.

'Look, we thought we were doing the right thing.'

Three heads nod.

'And we thought you'd know if that's true. Or if we are in trouble.'

'What do you think you did wrong?' I prod.

'Well, you know I said he wasn't dead after the fall?'

He waits for my response, but I don't want to interrupt. Red takes a great breath and prepares to get on with what he is here to tell and ask. Then I realise I need more about what he's just said. 'How did you know he wasn't dead?'

'Well, he was still bleeding. You don't bleed if you are dead, do you?'

I shrug my agreement.

'Get on with it, Red,' says George, irritated and irritating as ever. Unable to wait for him she stands, too.

'We thought it was better to get him home, you know, where he could be looked after.'

'What? So, none of you could be blamed?'

'I shouldn't have had the party,' whines Nigel D-B. 'We needed to clean up. You know, get rid of blood stains on the planter and carpet – and stuff like that, do y'see? The oldies were back in the morning. I'd be dead if they knew, do y'see?'

I twist away from him as nausea cramps my torso and I swallow scalding vomit. Housekeeping and spotless reputations before medical care for Richard? Any sympathy I have for naïve teenagers faced with an injured friend evaporates but an emotional response won't help.

'So are we in trouble, that's what we want to know,' shouts George.

'Trouble? Well, let's see. You thought you'd be in dead trouble because you had a party. A friend is injured with a deep head wound, is unconscious, bleeding and for all you know could soon be truly dead. Instead of calling an ambulance you agree it's more important to clean up the house and keep your party a secret? Is that it?'

There's implacable silence from four pale faces. The idea of moral responsibility over selfishness has no purchase.

'OK, so what did you do?'

George speaks up.

'The boys put him in a gardening bag and, well, then a wheelbarrow.'

'You wheeled him home on a barrow?'

'We covered up the bag with bottles and party stuff.'

'Anyone who saw us thought we'd started the Carnival early.'

'And then?'

Red shrugs, and his expression shows his relief at getting the shared truths out. 'We waited until there was no-one around and then dumped him on his doorstep.'

'Dumped?'

'Didn't mean to drop him but the plastic was slippery and he was heavy,' explains Nigel.

'But we rang the doorbell,' Charlie adds. 'We didn't just leave him there, did we?' She spreads her palms and it's pathetic to see the others do the same, as through expecting a reward for a good deed.

'And then?'

'Went back and finished clearing up.'

'Did anyone answer the door?'

'Didn't wait to see, did we?' exclaims George, astonished at my question.

'Not very nice,' I say. 'You thought you'd done the right thing and so that was that? Is that it?'

There's confusion on their faces. I suspect there is

little morality understood other than what is best for each of them. I will lull them into false comfort, hoping that conscience and decency will worm their way into their thinking and at last give them a bad time.

'I see your thinking,' I say, pretending to placate them. I am revolted by the looks of relief, as though blame is now dissolved.

'But are we in trouble?' Red and Nigel D-B ask together.

I pretend to think, pausing long enough to encourage hope of something favourable.

'Not for me to say, is it?'

There's universal astonishment and regret.

'We thought you'd know,' they chorus.

'You don't want to know what I think,' I say and herd them down the stairs and out of my deli.

What I'm thinking is how entitled and devoid of understanding they are of anything but their immediate wants or needs.

I christen them the Four MustGetTheirs.

Chapter 28

•

Thursday December 21st, 1978

Christmas Day is a Monday this year and today is the last Thursday before this. The deli is open late tonight, Friday and Saturday and will close at 4pm om Sunday.

Today is when most last-minute treats and gifts will be bought by locals going north, south, east and west to spend the weekend plus the 25th and 26th with Mummy and Daddy, with new or old lovers, or to do duty with aged relatives from whom they have expectations.

Those staying in London will shop later for their treats, most of which have been pre-ordered.

A bitter wind scarifies Portobello Road, but nothing must get in the way of Christmas sales. Most of the shop front is closed and the pavement chairs and tables are stored away. Instead, trestle tables are staffed by padded-up colonials and piled high with Polish plums in chocolate (as good but much cheaper than Carlsbads), with Pruneaux d'Agen, marrons glaces, French petits pois and Czech Pilsener Urquell, the original bottom-fermented lager. Throughout are beribboned boxes of Dan's Deli filled chocolates, always disappointing French glace fruits that sell at prices I can't justify, those Portuguese sardines in olive oil, Spanish ventresca tuna and Dan's Deli own-label wines, Vin Ordinaire and a more expensive

Premier Cuvee range. Lots of our own Christmas mince tarts and striped peppermint sticks and gingerbread tree decorations from Poland, too.

The outdoor selection is to help those who know nothing about finer foods and would be overwhelmed by the greater choice in the shop. Those who do know can make a quick selection without having to brave the scrum on the deli floor.

Jeremy has compiled a festive tape with little specific Christmas music. You won't hear Jingle Bells or White Christmas here. It's more Nutcracker Suite and those many determined Vivaldi concertos.

He and Luciana are on high alert for robbers and not just the kids who are targeting us. Some of the most persistent shop lifters are the best dressed and best spoken. Hard to say if these ladies and gentlemen have long-term mental challenges or are burdened with a sense of entitlement born of genteel poverty that in turn feeds a belief that they deserve what they cannot afford or should have bought for them. So, they take what they want. I learned a hard lesson through ignoring Richard Metcalfe's predations and have no mercy.

Miss Kitchen-Tat, a local bitch-shopkeeper of rip-off Casa Pupo ceramics and erudite cooking paraphernalia, swanks past the trestles, grabbing two mince pies as she does. 'I'll pay for these later,' she pipes in her affected voice that doesn't quite hide her North London ethnicity.

It's a last straw.

A hundred yards away she's opened a Christmas

Food Fayre under her shop without a word, whereas for years I had agreed never to sell any kit that's kitchen and cooking related. Jeremy's sister wanted to sell culinary antiques outside the deli on Saturdays, but Miss Kitchen-Tat had blocked it, 'so we never compete.'

'This woman is never to be served in this shop again!' I shriek over the chatter and tills and music. She interprets this as welcome attention just as Mrs Cheesecake would and grins as she leaves, still holding the pies.

'Last person who should be eating those,' says sharp Mrs Andrews, pointing at Miss K-T's undulating buttocks.

'Like watching a bleedin' storm at bleedin' sea,' a passing council street sweeper shouts after her.

That breaks the ice and shopping starts again but it stings that others are buying from the Food Fayre as well. Or instead. There'll be a come-uppance.

By 6pm the first of those who've finished work are streaming in from the 52-bus stop on Kensington Park Road or who have walked down from the Underground at Notting Hill Gate or over from Ladbroke Grove.

I'm adding orange slices to the mulled wine I offer to relax the retail-reticent when Trev shouts. 'Watch out, Boss!'

He's pointing across to Elgin Crescent. Meredith is hurtling towards us, aflap in ethnic woollens and with a trail of indigenous scarves tangling behind her. She's pulling Jem's resistant hand and is tugged at by a tearful Lena, still in pinafore and backless pom-pom slippers.

'You invaded us!' Meredith screams, feet planted in the gutter. Her eyes glitter and her metal frames reflect our festive lights.

'How dare you! Even the police need permission, you piece of shit!' She takes a huge stride onto the pavement and shoves Jem towards me, pincering his collar in a furious fist.

'Jem's outraged! You've raped him.'

Jem cringes and hides his head, but Meredith has more.

'It's rape to invade a teenage boy's bedroom.'

The charge is outrageous. I smile, which does nothing to cool her. Lena tries to tug Jem away, but Meredith pushes her with all her pent-up fury. Lena stumbles as one of her feet slides out of its slipper. Jem reaches to save her but both fall onto a trestle. There's a clattering Christmas kaleidoscope of sound and light as wine and lager bottles shatter on the pavement. The multi-coloured flood fizzes with gas from the lager and Christmas-gift flotsam floods the pavement.

Luciana and Jeremy force Meredith back into the gutter with a battlement of outstretched arms. She's oblivious to the bubbling liquids dribbling over her feet. 'It's not appropriate. You had no permission . . .'

'Did you have permission to break these bottles? Should you have raped that table?' Luciana is merciless as she towers over Meredith. 'You'll pay you know – and for loss of profit.'

Lena has struggled to her feet and is now supported by Jeremy. Her bare, chilled arms have been cut on broken wine and beer bottles, shards are still held in the folds of her face. She's dazed with shock, trembling and tearful. Jem landed on boxes of chocolates and cellophane-wrapped gingerbreads, so is shaken but not injured.

Jeremy holds Lena and picks away the biggest fragments, saying she will bleed less if she stays in the cold.

Just as when I was threatened with a knife, customers and staff are rigid and silent. I need to stop punters leaving without buying what's in their baskets and what else might have been.

'Princess Luciana, please take everyone upstairs. Trev, carry up the mulled wine.'

I'm sad to see how many staff join the grateful customers. Not the thing you experience in the Aussie outback, I suppose. Most customers also follow the spiced wine, excited to be hosted by a princess. Orlando encourages them, anxious for any to believe he is co-hosting with his friend Princess Luciana. The immune shuffle home through the frigid air.

Meredith is rigid at the impasse, impotent at being ignored rather than at shame for what she has done. There's no point talking to her.

'Sorry if you're upset, Jem,' I say. 'It's all to do with your friend Freddy. I'm trying to help. You know that, don't you?'

Threatened by his mother's iced eyes, he dares a quick glance at me. I think it's a plea, but for what?

'She's a pot head,' he says, unable to control rage. 'Out of control.'

'What's her problem?'

Jem struggles to speak and then there's that pleading in his eyes again. When he can, he whispers. 'Me,' he says. 'And, it's . . . it's complicated.'

Mr-Neatnik Trev has left Luciana to serve the wine upstairs and rushes to sweep the broken glass and alcohol into the gutter and to separate wine-damaged goods from those that might still be sold. I want to get Meredith away in case police fire themselves up to attend. She is screaming again.

'Do you think rape is appropriate? Breaking in . . .'

'Do you think this is appropriate?' I interrupt. 'If you have a problem with me, shouldn't you go to the police? They might interpret my visit as being a good neighbour.'

'It's home invasion! Rape of a teenage boy's bedroom. Anyway, I don't want to go to the police.'

'Because?

'Because you know how hopeless they are, and it takes too long and . . .'

'And who knows what else they might find there?'

'Like what!'

With great deliberation I mime smoking a spliff, nipping the usual soggy butt-end between my index finger and thumb. I take a slow pull and hold my breath, pretending almost to explode before expelling a long hiss between my teeth.

Pale and frightened, Meredith backs away from the gutter, still ignoring Trev's sweepings over her feet and his muttering at her. The throbs of my biggest Christmas star reflect on her spectacle frames. She could be a ticking bomb.

Luciana returns and gets right to it. 'Speaking of police, shall I telephone, Mr Heath?' she asks, eyes pooled with innocence.

'I'm going,' Meredith grunts.

'Do what you like,' says Luciana with withering indifference. 'You've committed Public Order offences and you've destroyed Mr Heath's beer and wine. And whatever else has fallen into it. That's wilful damage – it's a sort of stealing, isn't it?'

Jeremy joins in. 'To say nothing of assault on this lady here. We all saw you. You'd better just piss off. Now now, woman!'

Meredith pivots, perhaps as confused as we are by the curious, doubled-up South African expression.

'Don't bother coming back,' Meredith shrills at Lena. 'That's ever! And say goodbye to any Christmas bonus, too!'

When Meredith sees Jem put an arm around Lena, she crumples. Her hair and scarves now knotted by the wind, she looks weak and vulnerable. I'm fighting rising feelings of sympathy.

'Jem's all I've got left. I can't let anything happen to him. It would kill me.'

She's appealing to Jem, but he is unmoved, instead concentrating on holding Lena as Jeremy takes the last of the glass from her arms. Meredith shuffles away, oblivious of her wine-red footprints, then turns one more time with invigorated defiance.

'I'd kill you – any of you – if you hurt him!' She can't keep up the bravado. She stares at Jem and I understand the word beseeching. Getting nothing from him she flings out her arms, like a pilgrim pleading at Lourdes.

'You have to understand. Jem has to understand. He is all I have left. The only one . . .'

Deep-throated sobs punctuate her retreat until all we can hear is Trev's muttering and sweeping and, in that hiatus, new questions arise.

Why does Meredith say Jem is all she has 'left'. What else has she lost? Perhaps the question is who else has she lost?

'I've got a question you might like to ask that maniac of a woman,' a low voice says behind me.

There's Gauloise on the air. I turn to see Long John Silver, whom I've discovered has a basement flat – a Garden Flat in these parts - opposite Meredith's house. He and Jem exchange quick acknowledgements.

'Oh, yes,' he says after a theatrical dart over both shoulders. 'You might like to ask her about her girlfriend.'

Jem gives a low cry, and bends double, as though stabbed. His voice cracks with the strength of certainty.

'She never had a girlfriend! She didn't. Didn't! Didn't'! Didn't!!!'

When Long John's eyes return from imploring the night sky, he tosses his head.

'Tell that to Julie's Bar!'

He throws up his hands. 'There. I've said what I've

said. There's nothing more.'

Except there will be, so we wait.

'Well. It's not for me, is it? Just saying, you know I've not seen the girlfriend around for a while, have I?'

There's silence because no-one wants to ignore Long John or to agree with him. He enjoys the frisson 'girlfriend' creates and before anyone knows what to say, he has his final words.

'I'm not a fool, am I? These things come in three. First, that Richard tart dead, then that nice Freddy found on a fire and, now, well . . . who's safe?'

As Long John's tendril legs slither him down Elgin Crescent, Jem screams. 'She never, she never!'

Mrs Andrews pokes me in the chest. 'The boy might be telling you the girlfriend wasn't a girl,' she says with a wink and a finger to her nose.

I can't absorb that because Lena forces herself free of Jeremy and transfigures from victim to saviour.

'You'd better come home with me, Jem. I'll ring your Mum.'

'She won't like it.'

'You want to go home to her?'

Chapter 29

The Victory Antiques Arcade can wait no longer.

Antiques? That's a laugh. Most of the stuff is vintage, if that. How many visitors to Portobello know the difference? If it's something they've seen in their grandmother's china cabinet, it'll be an antique to them. I reckon most are no older than the 50s, plus some art deco and art nouveau. Well, 'style of' those, anyway.

Still, with experience, if you look hard and know what you want there are treasures. I hope to get out into the market for at least an hour every Saturday. Last week I scored four Irish linen table napkins woven with the heraldry of the countries of the British Empire for the coronation of George V and Queen Mary in 1911. Proper antiques they are, because they are over a century old, the goal-post definition that changes every year. And a bargain because the young seller had no idea who George V and Mary were or what the Empire was.

Yes, I did take advantage, profiting from ignorance and sloth. Just as most Saturday visitors to Portobello Road know little about what they see, many of the street stallholders know little about what they sell.

There are tricks to shopping in the market, inside and outside and I'll tell you about them some time.

Portobello Road on Saturday is one of London's greatest entertainments. The stalls set out on either side of the street offer everything imaginable from baby rattles to old cutlery to prints, silver and brass, genuine and fake. Few visitors buy, so only the most determined go into a shop or arcade where there are more specialist dealers, offering ancient tapestry fragments, Roman or Art Deco glass or out-of-print books on whatever you imagine.

Over the polyglot buzz you still hear old-fashioned market patter and calls and the jingle of a foot-worked tambourine accompanying a singer with a guitar, in turn attached by string to a wearied dog. Jugglers seem to shout loudest. The best I've seen ends his routine with a half a baguette onto which he has juggled a saucer and then a cup landed upright. Petit dejeuner en plein air he says.

By the afternoon the greater eccentrics have roused themselves. Like the skinny but well-built middle-aged bloke in a bowler hat and bare to the waist who tap dances while inviting the public to imprison him in yards of heavy chains and to padlock those. Within minutes he escapes and is collecting coins in a beret. I've heard more than one wonder why he doesn't spend the money on replacing a few of his teeth.

Like so many on Portobello Road, the Victory's entrance seems more the barricaded gatehouse to a castle, entrance achieved only after negotiating a moat of stalls on the pavement. Battling between them can elicit enough huffs and puffs from stern, seated sellers to put you off.

No arcade is well-lit and the first assault is on your nostrils. There's a universal thickness in the air that holds disturbing tokens of age. Rusty, mouldy, damp and dusty. Not unexpected I suppose considering what's for offer.

There's a sadness in the smell because it's not the well-tended ageing of polish and daily love. It's neglect, dirt and ignored dust, and the piercing, moist remnants of burned town-gas and greasy gas rings.

The gloomy ambiance is uneasy, everywhere reflected in the vacant faces of the stall holders in their overstuffed nests, who seem never to expect customers and are then suspicious of any who does approach. If it's true they've done most business with other dealers before 6am, are they just keeping watch that nothing is stolen during the day?

The Victory is on two floors. There is nothing and no-one to interest me on the ground, except discarded Dan's Deli paper bags, even though I don't recognise many customers.

There are two stairways to the basement and I take the back one. I creep down, feigning interest in nothing but using peripheral vision to identify where my attention should be, a technique taught by a chemistry teacher at school and that saved me from many an ambush in foreign bars, streets and markets.

The dealers down here seem more serious and to have better stuff. In front of me a whiff of moth balls predicts a stall of vintage clothes, men's and women's. What luck. It's Araminta, the one guest at the Guy Fawkes party none of us has spoken to. She's neat, tall and thin, with a widow's hump and white hair in a French roll, her face powdered but with no other makeup. There's an inner sparkle to her that's warming but it manages also to tell you she's not keen on whatever you call the fashion equivalent of tyre kicking.

A perfume ring is on a low-amp lamp, dispensing a faint vapour I distinguish as one of the older scents from Floris in Jermyn Street, a clean cologne but with rose and jasmine. Very classy and in period with what I see she is selling and wearing.

Araminta wears a floral print in navy and white, pre-WWII I judge by the fitted bodice, padded shoulders, cap sleeves, Peter Pan collar, belted waist and flared skirt. You absorb such knowledge without thinking in Portobello Road.

She wears pince-nez and is busy sorting through the drawer of a sewing box. She selects four floral diamante buttons which she arranges on a scarlet velvet evening jacket spread flat on the table that cuts her off from the narrow passage between stalls.

'Looks like a good choice,' I observe.

'Do you think so?' she beams, and then leans back with her eyes narrowed. Her pince-nez drops but not far because it is suspended by a black silk cord attached to a gold stud on her left shoulder.

'Oh. It's you. Yes, Meredith said I should expect you?'

'Why was that?'

'Well, you know, that poor boy on the fire.'

'Oh, nothing to do with that,' I pretend. 'I've realised I know little of what goes on in the arcades and I'm taking time off, even though Christmas is coming.

'Oh Christmas! I'm so busy with my alterations and such . . . you can imagine.'

'That's what you do, more than just sell these wonderful things?' I ask, running my hand over an overlapping rainbow waterfall of beaded flapper dresses that hang ceiling to floor.

'Wonderful things like this don't just happen, you know, Mr Heath. That's what Meredith always . . .'

'Meredith is involved?'

'She's a marvel. She doesn't have a stall but deals from home and that includes finding me dresses to repair. She's a whizz at haberdashery, too, always ferreting out the right sort of buttons and labels.'

There's that word again.

'Why labels?'

'It's naughty I know but you're in business. You'll understand. Sometimes I sew in better labels. The best are from the 40s and 50s. Golden years.'

'To get a better price?'

'Exactly.'

'I've always loved labels,' I enthuse. 'My mother taught me that. Even if nobody can see them, it makes you feel better.'

'Exactly. Would you like to see some?'

Without waiting, Araminta plucks a handful from a drawer and scatters them in front of me.

I recognise the greatest. Chanel and Dior, Hardy Amies, Balenciaga, Norman Hartnell, Balmain, Digby Morton. Digby Morton? Really? Then, it's there. There's a Rahvis label but I dare not pounce.

Chapter 30

I murmur the famous names as I turn the labels over on Araminta's stall and when I pretend to discover the Rahvis again, I exclaim.

'My mother's favourite! She always had Rahvis.'

'Sisters they were, or is it are? Rae and Dora. Almost the only successful women in fashion. I still know Rae. Just as famous for the glass dining table in her Mayfair apartment. No footsie there.

'They did movie costumes, too,' she adds. Aha. That makes even more sense of the dress Richard was wearing.

'My mother loved that connection,' I lie. 'So glamorous. . .'

I sigh, my eyes downcast. What a ham, but the ends justify the whatisname, don't they? 'What memories something like this would bring her and what pleasure. Do you sell them?'

'Oh yes, others rename too. But only if I'm sure the garment has the quality, of course.'

'I'd love to buy it for her.'

'It's just come in,' she says, a common ploy of dealers as they wonder what they dare charge. 'I haven't thought about a price. It cost me quite a bit . . .' Blah blah I continue in my mind.

'I don't mind. It's priceless to me.'

We agree a sum and I tuck the label into my pocket,

'Is it indiscreet to ask how you got it? Did it come on a frock that was too damaged to repair?'

'No, just as it is but with others. From Meredith, last week. She's a brilliant forager. I hope your mother will be impressed you tracked down a Rahvis label.'

It's not my long-dead mother I want to impress. It's Luciana and Trev. Is it the label from Richard's last party frock? Has Meredith found it by accident? Or did she cut it off? Even if it weren't her, I bet she knows who did. Pity she won't talk to me.

I'm making my way to the forward steps and today's luck is still with me. In a gloomy corner, even less well-lit than other stalls, is Barry the ex-Sports Teacher, fenced in by old racquets, clubs, boots and sports programmes but doing something quite unrelated.

I develop an interest in a stall specialising in old newspapers, some of them 18th and early 19th century. Perhaps I am wrong about the age of what is sold here? I hope that while pretending interest in how English papers reported Napoleon's doings I can decipher Barry's real interests.

While I appear to read, young boys and girls come and go and yes some of them are my snotty shoplifters. Others are teenage youths, just, and every one of them hangs a cigarette from his lips. Each delivers an envelope or parcel, or is given one to deliver. A coin is slipped into their hand each time they do.

I get it. It's a Portobello messenger and delivery service, so stall holders can communicate without leaving their stands or stalls to find a telephone, and then collecting and delivering items others want to buy or sell. Bet they pay well for the service.

Nothing sinister in that, is there? Or can I not see it?

Then Araminta is beside me, herself holding a parcel.

'Still here I see.' She interprets my startled look as a question. 'Me? Oh, I'm just taking something to Barry over there,' she explains. 'He'll soon get it delivered for me.'

There's nothing for it but innocence. 'I was just going to say hello to him,' I say and take her elbow.

'So this is how it works is it, Barry? Wondered why I hadn't seen you in the deli for a while. Must keep you very busy.'

It's Araminta who answers. 'Sometimes I think Portobello would seize up without the service he gives. This frock will be in Westbourne Grove in hours.'

I turn to Barry. 'But aren't your messengers too young to work?'

'Keeps them out of trouble,' Araminta says. 'Better than them shop-lifting and Heaven knows what else these days. It's our little secret and it must stay that way.'

There's a definite implication of threat, however, I also see a curious logic because it seems everyone is winning.

I remember why I am here.

'Was Richard Metcalfe ever involved?' I ask.

'His brilliant idea, wasn't it? Years ago, when he was just 10 or 11.' Araminta looks into the distance and then says, 'Imagine what that boy could have done if he lived.'

For a split-second Barry and my eyes meet in grudging agreement but I suspect we have with different ideas of what the outcome might have been. I see an opportunity to knot together some thoughts.

'So, the shoplifting these kids do in my deli is to 'encourage' me to keep the secret of this message network – and the money it makes. You think the more I know about Richard and how he died the more you and it might be in danger?'

'It's the only job I can get,' Barry whispers and he blushes.

I guess the rest. There's more to his dismissal from St Benedict's. If the messenger network is secret, his sexual meanderings stay so, too. My investigating of Richard's death risks both exposing the child labour of the network and more about his past. That's why I am being threatened. And where does the Man in Black figure in this more and more complicated web?

I'm about to ask when I see a safe almost hidden in the corner and another jack falls into a pot or whatever you're supposed to say.

Could that be where Richard kept his cash, wherever it came from? Do Belinda and Johnny know about the safe?

What else is in there? How can I get into it?

Jeff springs to mind.

Chapter 31

•

December 24th, 1978

How often must I remind myself that it's the clue under my nose that is the hardest to spot? Or that I must remember to ask the next question. Not to accept something is there but to ask why it is there. And so on.

It's 8am Sunday morning, December 24th, Christmas Eve. The deli will heave with last-minuters because I'll close at 4pm. My mind will heave too if our mysteries don't get solved, hence this need to talk things out.

I've gathered Luciana, Trev and Jeff over croissants, smoked salmon, Westphalia's black-skinned smoked ham, pickled cucumbers and Italian Mostarda di Cremona. Luciana relishes the extreme heat that mustard oil gives the syrup supporting those sweet, crystallised fruits. It's heat and sweet in extremis and I've never found the flavours bridge to make something coherent, as in sweet and sour recipes. Why would anyone want to eat something very expensive that attacks the mucus in your eyes and nose while being chewed? One more Italian mystery.

'What don't we know?' I ask as I pour coffee and hot milk, adjusting the mix for each large cup according to preference. Mugs are forbidden in this house and Trev is still uneasy with saucers.

'Richard first,' I say.

'I reckon we can trump something up to get that safe opened,' Jeff offers. 'Suspicion of dope dealing always works. Gets us into all sorts of interesting places.'

'Between now and New Year?'

'Boys will be pleased to have something to do other than refusing to help with annoying house alarms or lounging around and playing house in upmarket flats and houses that have been burglarised while the owners are away.'

Trev likes that idea and wants to know more, but Luciana widens her eyes a little to stop that. They've developed an astonishing rapport across the chasm between their ages and social origins. But Trev isn't being shut up.

'Look, Boss, that next question thing you goes on about. What about that sausage machine?'

'Must we?' grimaces Luciana, stuffing a croissant with smoked salmon. I'm happy to see she has sliced it open with a serrated knife and no pressure rather than wrecking it. How do people choose a pastry made to be light and flaky but attack it with a blunt table knife and then squash it?

'World of Dan' is how some dismiss me when I pontificate over the food ignorance of others, as though I am the only one who thinks like this. I'm not, am I?

Trev gets us focussed. 'Yes, princess, we gotta talk about sausages,' he says. '

I interrupt, seeing where he is going. 'Right, we do because we doesn't (I correct my Trevism) don't know what it means, or what someone was planning.'

'Yeah, all that Boss. How about this as the next question? Who knew how to operate the sausage maker? You thought of that?'

'Bloody Hell, Trev. You've made this worthwhile already.'

'Fanks,'

'I've warned you,' scolds Luciana.

'Sorry, thanks.'

'What's that coffee ever done to you?' I ask Jeff. He's been stirring it for ages, clanging the spoon on the cup sides.

'Apologies, a thinking thing. Both those lads had been dead for a while, hadn't they? Richard for a couple of days and, well, who knows about Freddy because he was deep frozen.'

I think I know where Richard was but as for Freddy, there's nothing in my mind and it's true I haven't thought about it.

'He must have been carried to Meredith and Jem's place. How do you do that? He hadn't been folded up, had he?' Jeff adds.

That hadn't occurred. It's relevant, so I share what I know about Richard, the wheelbarrow and all that. There's agreement it worked because he was alive and could be bent and folded. By the time he was put in my kitchen, rigor mortis would be over and he'd be flexible again.

What could have carried Freddy lying flat or standing up if his body was frozen stiff?

'The back of a van. Or one of those tall, two-wheeler

trolleys used in the market?' suggests Jeff.

My mind flies to what Lena revealed about Freddy's conception and those overnight storage units behind Portobello's fruit and veg market. How secure are they? Could someone nick a trolley from there and, another thought, do they have deep freezers? Is that where Freddy was stored?'

'Shall I take a walk down the market and ask?' Luciana offers.

'They'll love that the day before Christmas!' I laugh, but we can spare her because she doesn't serve. The rest of us will be taking money. Even Jeff, who loves selling cheese.

'I'll pretend I'm worried for them because of the long break,' she explains. 'Anyway, there are few out. Most said arrivederci to Brussels sprouts yesterday.'

'Better do that before the rush,' I say, slicing more smoked salmon, one of my special skills. Now's not the time to explain that, but I will sometime. 'What else?'

Jeff's in fast. 'That girlfriend business and Meredith.'

'Jem hated that, didn't he?' says Luciana.

'And Long John Silver was adamant. What did he say? Ask them at Julie's. I've never got over there – any of you get over Holland Park way?'

'Tim and Cathy Herring are good friends and changing life in their little village,' says Luciana. 'Easy for me to ask.'

'Hold on,' says Jeff. 'Isn't that where your friend Helen goes, Dan?'

'Works there sometimes,' I agree.

Bloody hell! That's something far too close to see. I haven't seen Helen for months, yet she could solve this in seconds. I agree to telephone her, if I can find her number.

I jot a note to do that and then see Jeff is diverted by a Polaroid of Jem's bedroom ceiling.

'Ever joined up the big dots?' he asks.

'Why would you do that,' Trev enquires.

Jeff reaches for a felt tip pen and draws careful lines on the print.

'Meaningless to me,' says Trev.

Luciana taps the Polaroid. 'It's a constellation.'

'What's that?'

'Obvious, Trev. A shape of stars. People always have seen things in them, like gods and animals, which I've never been able to do. Use them as birth signs and predictions, telling the future.'

'What, like them crystal ball things?' Trev is mocking.

'Horoscopes,' Jeff answers.

'Exactamente!' Luciana agrees. 'But which one?'

'Easy, princess,' says Jeff. 'It's Gemini.'

'And when it's at home?' Trev cheeks.

'The Heavenly Twins, Castor and Pollux.'

I don't need tickets to tell me this is an invitation for Trev to joke about bollocks. Just as my hand stops him, Jeremy yells up that there's a crowd outside the deli and he wants to open early.

At last. I'm feeling the Batman buzz that's been missing, sense myself back on those downhill skis. I know Jeff has thrown a major clue into the melting pot but can't assess it yet.

Right now, I'm wanted to serve up smoked salmon to order for countless Notting Hillbilly Christmas tables. Not just do that but use my knife skills to create thin slices from the full length of the side. I've given up telling anyone it tastes better when it's thick, but they want to see the plate through it and that's what they get. It's more a floor show I do towards the front of the deli om Saturdays, because it attracts people who might otherwise walk past.

Yes, I know, it's Sunday but it's Christmas Eve and what's that deli-lectable sound I'm hearing?

Oh yes, Jingle Jingle.

That's cash registers in my ears, not sleigh bells.

...

Christmas selling is over, and Jeremy has binned his music tapes to the relief of the shop floor. The classical music has been, well, music to most of my customers but its repetition has been jangling rather than jingling to the staff.

He is tidying, pulling forward bottles, cans and packets so the shelves look full and neat, well needed after the sad rush of the past hour. We stayed open until 4.30 selling chocolates, Stilton and Port to those who discovered they were not going to be alone and slicing ham and smoked salmon for those accepting a solo Christmas. Jeremy then took his battalion of colonials for a big drink with Gabriel at the wine bar up the hill.

Luciana and I make desultory attempts to help the clear up but it's not her thing and my feet are thumping. I open a bottle of Palo Cortado, a rare sherry with the rich mouth feel and caramel-gold sheen of a sweet cream variety but with a dry and chewy finish. Very satisfying after a hard day's graft. I always keep a couple in the Cheese Cabin, so they are chilled but not ice-cold because that would mask the subtleties.

Jeff left selling cheese earlier and comes back with news the safe in the Victory will be opened but it's better if we don't know more. He and Trev do a High Five, that new thing that has crossed the Atlantic faster than a Jumbo Jet.

All afternoon, Luciana has nursed a curious smile, and even been helping customers with their shopping. I expect it's because amidst the clatter she's made jewellery sales. She still has a chute of five diamond stars ascending in diminishing sizes in her hair, so it wasn't one of them. This morning she asked if I thought they were too Empress Sissi and was miffed when I didn't know who that was. The assassinated second-to-last Empress of Austria-Hungary. Apparently.

I open a Camembert Fermier that's too perfect not to eat with butter, Bath Olivers and a few olives. Luciana is still smiling and making noises I identify as snickers. Must have been some sale.

'Freezers in those old garages?' I ask, thinking she might have made a special discovery she's longing to share.

'No. But yes. Very easy to get hold of a trolley.'

She takes her time walking to the Cheese Cabin, not to her stool outside it but inside it, and then emerges with an expensive-looking carrier bag on gold chains. Discreet lettering says it is from Rome's uber-fancy Via Condotti.

Luciana tests us by keeping the carrier shut and protracts the anticipation by putting it between her feet and cutting another wedge of Camembert and making unnecessary adjustments to her festoon necklace of moonstones and garnets. She doesn't know I've bagged it for next year's Christmas tree.

'Lovely,' she says, emptying her glass of Palo Cortado. 'Molto soddisfacente.' We hope that means something good.

At last, she opens the bag. The contents are not from Rome.

'Time for La Principessa to invite some people in, I think,' she says. 'Non è vero, Signor Deli-Detective Dan?'

She might not know the word, but Luciana is gloating.

Big time.

She deserves it.

PART THREE
SERVED UP

December 1978 to January 1979

Chapter 32

•

December 26th, 1978

Boxing Day is always about me, me seeing no-one and doing nothing. More so now I have the deli. Today, the swirling mind and smouldering feet both need attention and a good rest before the forthcoming furore of catering for New Year's Eve customers.

I've a warmed Sara Lee Pecan Coffee Cake in the oven and am pulling at it from time to time. Yes, you're right. I plan to absorb all of it, together with occasional bacon and constant coffee. It's something I do every Boxing Day morning.

There's no interruption from upstart Capital Radio. No classy Radio 3. Not even soothing Nina Simone or smoothie Nat King Cole on the Bang & Olufsen turntable.

All I have planned is to telephone Helen. Luciana used her connections to trace her through Julie's, the starry Holland Park restaurant where she sometimes works. I intend to apologise for seeming to desert her. On the other hand, she hasn't contacted me, but I hope that is a good thing, that she has found a new life.

Helen is a life saver.

We met during our cancer treatments and teamed up because our side effects gave us common grounds.

Losing a breast in her 30s created problems for her perceptions of femininity, just as testosterone suppression threatened my masculinity.

Helen became my lodger, and we slept in the same bed for more than a year, sustained by the privilege of intimate trust that didn't need to be proved with sex. Neither of us had the self-confidence or ability to share a sexual relationship but we both needed profound reassurance of our identity. Lots of spooning.

As an apparent couple we built a wall that protected our inner outrage and rawness from any intrusion of the outside world, and this helped us to step back into it.

Remember that time she and Jeff walked in together on the Saturday after Freddy was found in the bonfire? Complete chance. They didn't know one another then and still don't, as far as I know.

There's no way Luciana can invite people before New Year's Eve. For one thing, it would be better if her event coincided with my annual entertainment that's a devious plan to appear generous to those who have been helpful – or who might be. That's done with lavish food and drink early in the New Year, but few guests know this is how my deli gets value from festive items I can no longer sell. If certain goodies don't move by the finish of party-time shopping on December 31st, they are fixtures and must be dumped or used.

I don't think food should be seen at marked-down prices, so I might as well get something out of it. I use it to flatter, influence and charm.

A few dozen orphan Christmas puddings are stored away for Easter, when there is an unexplained surge for them. The remainder are crumbled and mixed with softened vanilla ice cream, orange-flower water and rosewater. Once refrozen, Dan's Christmas Pudding Ice Cream becomes a signature of my catering for as many months as it lasts, which is not many.

This New Year happening, or party as we used to say, will also set up some sleuthing. The agenda is to reveal what we know about the deaths of Golden Dick and Freddy the Fire, hoping this will force others to tell us something we don't know. DS Jeff will make sure DI Harding is there, so I don't seem to be treading on his toes, even though it seems Harding has forgotten the two dead boys.

There's no solid evidence against anyone yet but there's every chance we'll be closer to suspects among the guests. We hope alcohol and loose talk will promote exposures, and these will help uncover the murderers. It'd be good to start the year without these burdens. Batman without Bat Signals.

It won't be a Poirot-like gathering of a few suspects in a smart country-house drawing room. There'll be fifty or more guests anxious to share the hospitality of an Italian princess in a Chepstow Villas palazzino. The numbers will help get rid of my surfeit of tinned quails' eggs, white peaches and lobster, of Stollen, and those dratted glace fruits and such.

Anyone with a conscience will be comforted into thinking they are safe in a crowd while being treated like Portobello royalty.

The combined stimuli of caffeine and the coffee-cake's sugar cannot stop me dozing, encouraged by the occasional slap of sleet across my windows. I'm in the right place. I hear this is the coldest winter since the 60s.

When the doorbell rings I'm tempted to stay snuggled under my musquash-fur rug on the chesterfield. My body has mapped and claimed a line of comfort between its lumps.

There's an insistence I cannot ignore but first I peep down at the street. It's Jeff and he's stressed. It's not a social call.

'That old lady you met over at the Victory,' he pants as he runs up the stairs. 'She's been attacked in the street.'

'Is it serious?'

'She mightn't make it. I thought – well, I wonder . . .'

'So do I. She was there bonfire night, is into old frocks and stuff like Richard was wearing, and knows about the Portobello children's network. Can I see her?'

'You can if you're with me.'

I shove cake and coffee at Jeff and leap upstairs to dress for a fast walk almost to the top of Portobello, where Araminta lives in one of the cute two-down, two-up cottages on the east side.

When still conscious, she refused to be taken away by ambulance. There's a uniformed copper inside the front door and out of the weather to deter further aggression. A nurse has been found to sit at her bedside.

It's more distressing to see injury on someone living than on the dead. Araminta's face is a clump of contusion and abrasion. One fragile arm and a leg are broken. Ribs too.

Yet there's something serene about her.

'Tranquillisers, pain killers and shock,' explains the nurse. 'She'll not think any of it is real.' The 'begorrah' she adds gives unsubstantiated confidence.

'I don't suppose she has said anything?' I ask, not expecting something positive.

'Holy Mother of God,' she says with multiple crossings of her starched bosom. 'Poor wee thing seems to think it's still Christmas Day. Listen, there she goes again.'

I bend close. Araminta does seem be sending good wishes.

'It won't be them terrible injuries what takes her from us to the loving arms of Jesus,' says the nurse. 'It'll be the shock of being attacked and falling, so it will. And at her front gate, too. Always makes it worse, so it does, it does. Just when she felt safe.'

'And look,' she adds close to my ear, I suppose because they say hearing is the last thing that goes in the dying.

'She's 82. Ambulance agreed not to take her to St Mary's because they didn't think she'd be with them when they arrived. Lovely Catholic boys from Kerry and Limerick they was. Jesus bless them for working on St Stephen's holy day.

'Together we thought it kinder to lay her in her own bed, so we did, and let her meet . . . Holy Mother of God, she's passing!'

A tremor is shaking Araminta and her eyes have

opened. With great clarity, she says, 'Merry, merry, merry.'

I hear myself pull in a sharp breath as she does. When we exhale, the air leaves me with a sense of loss.

I open my eyes to find Araminta is dead.

My predictable tears are not just of sadness. They are also for the irony that battered Araminta's final words were of kindness, wishing others a good Christmas. Through this miasma of black emotions, a more frightening thought hurls itself forward.

Is this the third murder predicted by Long John Silver?

Could I be next?

Jeff puts a steadying hand on my shoulder as I shiver and stumble. Once I am settled, he says we should look around Araminta's cottage while we can.

It's old-world gentility. Rather too much good, inherited furniture, topped by bleached linen squares and circles bordered with froths of fine tatting or crochet. Nice watercolours in intricate frames worth more than their contents. A china cabinet, of course, with beeswax and lavender in the air.

When Jeff lifts a faded kilim thrown over what we expect to be a chest in a hall alcove, we discover a freezer. It's anachronistic and there's more to surprise us. It's stuffed with old clothes. I pick at them, lifting vintage tuxedos, embroidered evening cloaks, and wedding veils, all folded between tissue paper, each stiff and hoary.

'Good housekeeping, that,' says the nurse, tippy-toeing between Jeff and me.

Jeff laughs. 'You'll have to explain that.'

'Kills them moths, to be sure.'

We both stare, perplexed.

'You puts 'em in the freezer when you buys old clothes from a market, you do. Or from somewhere foreign. For a month they reckon. Kills the gobshites' eggs, so it does.'

'Prevents 'em laying new ones, too,' I suppose.

'Without the yuk of moth balls,' adds Jeff. 'Clever.'

The call has been made. With the constable at the door and the nurse by Araminta's bedside, there's no need for us to wait for the undertaker and his box.

Not the Boxing Day Araminta expected.

Chapter 33

•

December 28th, 1978

It's been a 'funnies' day. They've all been in. Jeremy doesn't know whether to laugh or to slit his throat.

The curious nothingness of the days between Christmas and New Year disturbs those who are less secure of mind, whatever their income. My interpretation is that their discomfort is constructed on an unrealised fear of not getting to Harrods or Harvey Nichols in time for New Year Sale goodies. My richest customers love a bargain, even if they don't need one.

Most of the 'funnies' are lonely and promote human interaction by complaining, dithering, demanding undeserved refunds, or to nag for something they've been told a hundred times we do not stock or cannot source.

Today they are also agog for details of Araminta's death and wondering which of them might be next, a welcome break from their normal concerns.

Jeremy tries to convince his colonials that tolerating them now will return these BPODs back into loyal customers when the apparent murder has been solved and they feel safer. Not all of them can see that far ahead, so he has been intervening hour after patient hour, hence his live/die dilemma.

Had you guessed? We give customers nick names and initial identities so we can chat amongst ourselves while we serve, even if one of them is being a pain on the deli floor.

OJB is the overweight Jewish bloke who thinks no-one knows he's gay. He wants meats and salami (should he be eating pork?) sliced to be transparent but won't accept any that look tattered. He takes longer to serve than anyone else because he stands over the slicer like a supervising surgeon, signalling yes and no with porcine grunts.

LJD is the charming, lisping Lithuanian Junk Dealer who operates a shop in the tatty section of Kensington Park Road that's just north of Elgin Crescent. It's a complete jumble, a permanent buzzy Saturday market and somehow the contents transform every few days. I've bought wondrous bargains there mid-week and then made hundreds of quid from selling them on because he doesn't know as much as he thinks.

LJD asks for aufschnitz, off cuts, perhaps because his trade hasn't been up to scratch, perhaps because he likes the variety. His purchases help our profits, balancing the wastage caused by OJB. We keep a bowl of trims, end pieces or mistakes made on the electric slicer, and sell the mixture cheap. Every time we do, I cross my fingers they are still safe to eat. When there are none, LJD stands determined until someone has sliced a little from every style of flesh we offer.

We should say no, or charge more rather than less.

Chubby OJB and skinny LJD survive with safe digestions, but the price paid by the shredded nerves of staff serving them, and of customers forced to wait, is disproportionate to what profit I take.

BPODs are a more regular challenge. These are the posse of elderly single or widowed women who straggle in after 4.30, once they have woken from a nap. BPOD stands for Back-Parting Old Dears, because they refresh their make-up and tidy their hair but forget to comb the back on which they have been resting. This leaves a clear divide, the back parting that amuses us, unkind as that might be. Some are sweet and are welcome customers. We better enjoy the departures of the whinging BPOD majority, who use the shop as therapy to help them through another day of sulking and regret. However, while they are together their competitive gossiping is aways amusing and I suspect might be useful in helping solve the Araminta mystery. She piled her hair up rather than combed it down, yet she was of their age and I imagine a heightened sense of vulnerability might elicit something useful. That's far from what's top of my mind right now.

My mind wants to sort out a different aufschnitz, the loose ends about Richard and Freddy. Like those meat off-cuts, some will be past their use, some will be worth digesting.

A To-Do list is needed, clarifying what I know and do not, in preparation for the planned party at Luciana's house up the hill.

1: Richard: I've established he was taken to Portobello Rd in a wheelbarrow and how he was injured.

Whodunnit, I underline, thinking of the slashes on his chest.

Who abandoned him in my deli kitchen?

What do the knife and the sausage machine mean?

How did he get there and why choose there?

Do the graffiti on the wall tiles help?

Who cut the label out of his dress and where are his gold heels?

2: Freddy: where and how did he die?

Where was he deep-frozen and why?

How did his frozen body get to Meredith and Jem's house?

What does Jem's starry ceiling mean and is it relevant?

3: Meredith: she seems a common thread but how and why?

Is her husband of interest?

Did she have a girlfriend?

If so, where is she now?

4: Araminta: complete mystery, even though she jig-saws into the life of Meredith and Barry.

There's more to know than these questions, including the whereabouts of deep-tanned Man in Black and I want to know what the raid found in Barry's safe.

Oh! Why doesn't Barry have a nickname? It doesn't take long to recognise this as a pointless cerebral diversion, a disabling eccentricity that I've never been able to conquer.

It's hard to tell you about it, but here goes. I go off into diversions because I don't like everything known and finished. I'm not comfortable when all is final, tidied, done and dusted. That goes as much as for a kitchen sink as it does for a To Do list about murder victims and suspects.

I must know or see there's something left to do and then ensure this weird comfort by ignoring what is obvious to others. Through many dramatic lurches I've understood with earthworm speed that I'm terrified of there being nothing to be done. When confronted by a pristine kitchen or faced with a void once a mystery is resolved, I feel I am abandoned, exposed in the middle of a deserted sports stadium, naked and with floodlights blazing.

It's a frightening feeling and I've come to understand it's because my greatest fear is of loneliness or of being pointless.

What's worse is the fear of being seen by others to be lonely or useless.

I'm nauseated and sweating as I tell you this but I'm deep breathing and hoping this does what it's supposed to do. The challenge ahead is whether I can follow through and get to the truth about Richard and Freddy and Araminta.

Or will I fudge and overlook something that would tidy up our cases, so that I have 'something to do'?

Chapter 34

January 6th, 1979

Luciana and I giggled for days. We chose Saturday January 6th for the New Year party before realising it is also the Feast of the Epiphany, the celebration of the three Magi visiting a newborn in a stable in Bethlehem with offerings of gold, frankincense and myrrh, whatever they are.

'Epiphany it will be indeed if we get the break-throughs we want,' I sniggered, amused by the happenstance of date.

'I'll make it a Magical Magi Stable Happening!' exclaimed Luciana. 'Did it years ago in Naples. Princess Maria-Constanza caught her golden halo in the dangling hand grip of her Cadillac El Dorado, couldn't free it, and was driven straight home with her neck at a very curious angle. Troppo divertente!'

'There won't be a lot of that, princess,' I laughed. 'Most of them will walk here.'

I might have said they'd arrive by Sputnik. Luciana's head was somewhere else and she then disappeared for most of the following days, except for the odd hour on her deli perch as she surveyed potential invitees or double checked our detecting.

You can imagine the 'I-don't-care-if-I-don't-get-invited' faces that shuffled closer to her once news of the happening circulated.

Luciana's palazzino is one of Chepstow Villas'

smaller detached houses, and that's using smaller in comparison to huge mansions. Hers is two floors of four expansive rooms over a raised basement, where the original kitchen space and staff accommodation are still used the ways they were planned, by her live-in cook Lucca and her housekeeper/maid Elena. Her first floor is a double drawing room on the right, mirrored by a morning room and dining room. The upper floor is also four rooms, a bedroom, a boudoir, an ex-bedroom divided into a walk-in wardrobe and luscious bathroom that secretes a jewel vault, and then a spare bedroom.

On Magical Magi night there are candles in every window, which is a seasonal Notting Hill and Holland Park thing anyway. Inside, beeswax tapers in crystal chandeliers and wall sconces light the first-floor rooms, all reflected to infinity in opposing looking glasses and on the marble floors.

Biblical Bethlehem is suggested by a tent in the morning room of rough woven wool furnished with bales of sweet hay and a couple of confused sheep tethered on patches of real turf. Rather startling to see among the ancient cassoni, priceless tapestries and Renaissance Old Masters.

'A few bibelots I gathered when I scappato, what you call bolted,' Luciana laughed as she waved a dismissive hand when I once dared to ask.

Each 'bibelot' would buy the deli building and is displayed against brocade-panelled walls and furnishings of dyed velvets and silks in profound heritage colours garish by day but sensational by candlelight, as they were meant to be seen.

It's been a late start, to give Portobello's invited shopkeepers, costermongers and stall holders time to recover from Saturday's fray, so it's 9 before most guests are here. Suits me of course, as I am preparing food in Luciana's basement kitchen, helped by her chef Lucca. The specialty tonight will be my revolutionary constructions of squares of filo pastry.

Instead of using the see-through sheets to wrap a pie or folding stuffed, paper-thin layers into shapes, I bake filo in unfettered small squares, each of six buttered layers that conflate like puff pastry on pot. Easy to divide into layers of three, I sandwich these with exotic mixtures and the contrast of texture is wondrous, even though there are complaints about how flakes drop everywhere.

'Be more careful,' I say with little sympathy.

I'm also cooling dozens of squares that have caster sugar added to the anointing butter between layers, so later I'll make Christmas pudding ice-cream sandwiches. Nouvelle Cuisine Heath, I like to think, even though I don't like to think about nouvelle cuisine at all. Not since a smart friend of mine exclaimed it meant 'embossed' plates and shouted about the size of a serving, saying, 'That's not fish, that's bait'.

The effort taken to dress up for the Magical Magi Stable Happening is wondrous. There are perhaps too many shepherds in kaftans and with tea towels tied about long hair. Sheets once used as ghost shrouds have become angels' robes, with or without wings or halos, and there's been much attention by Long John

Silver and his special friends to appear as the Magi. Draped brocade and velvet robes with sequinned passementerie worn over voluminous trousers and crowned with jewelled turbans, that sort of thing.

Very much what I have done, too, except that my en tremblant diamond-and-sapphire turban sarpech is real, thanks to Luciana's collections.

When I explained these words to Trev he guffawed at me for speaking that 'foreign lingo', but I reminded him this was the good stuff he went on about and that if there were English words they would be used in the Portobello, where I learned them. Well, there and standing beside Luciana at Old Bond Street and Burlington Arcade windows. Doesn't passementerie sound more interesting than saying braids and trims and tassels?

Meredith is snide and dismisses all Magi robes, including mine, as ex-curtains but then she's made little effort, wearing a vintage embroidered Jordanian robe that has vague geographical reference to the Magical Magi theme. I think her constant put-downs are good reason for any shepherd to be in a field rather than at home, but keep that to myself.

The Metcalfes wear black. 'I'm mourning a son, so dressing up to mark the birth of someone else's doesn't seem right,' Belinda declared when she arrived.

Luciana is wearing revised jewels, in the constant way of the late Queen Mary, the queen's imperious grandmother. Her five diamond stars plus other pieces have become a dazzling pageant of gemstones paraded on knife-edge pins that float high on a circlet wrapped in alternating folds of gold velvet and silk. It's not quite a halo, not quite the Queen of Heaven (she is in spangled dark blue) but most would get the implication.

'If not me, who?' she had asked.

Just as we both feel satisfied all is settling, there is an insistent doorbell.

'Bit determined,' I say to Luciana.

'Vulgar,' she sniffs.

Chapter 35

It's hard to credit who we see. It's Miss Kitchen-Tat, the uninvited back-stabbing proprietor of Christmas Fayre. I can just see her annoying simper through the bows of an over-ribboned hamper.

'I thought you'd like something for your party. I'm saying sorry, you know, for my Christmas Fayre.'

Thinking this is enough, she is toeing her way from the colonnaded porch and through the door, slitty eyes flashing as she checks both who is seeing her and who she sees.

'Happy New Year, Luciana,' she coos.

'That's Princess Luciana!' This is loud enough for most to turn to see who was being snubbed. Undaunted, Miss K-T steps back and undulates the hamper over her hips and thighs and on to the tiled porch floor.

'There, I bet that's worth a ticket in,' she crows, prying back the top.

Luciana, Jeremy and Trev join me to eye the contents, like lionesses assessing prey. We see a mean selection of Christmas Fayre leftovers, all second rate before December 25th and worthless now.

Noble suppliers of fine foods protect their customers by never selling to a neighbouring competitor. What Miss K-T managed to assemble from the ignoble is seasonal novelties aimed at punters far less sophisticated than the ones she hoped to attract from Dan's Deli.

'Your proposal is?' Luciana demands.

Interpreting this as meaning she and her hamper were welcome, Miss K-T simpers harder. 'Oh, that I add these to Dan's leftovers and help make sure there's enough for everyone to eat. As I said, it's a little apology.'

Jeremy claps his hands and bellows in best military Blonde Beast style to ensure the attention of our guests.

'This lady,' he begins, but is interrupted by an unladylike snort from Luciana. 'Yeah, correction, this person thinks we might not have enough to eat. And that we are being offered stingy leftovers by Mr Heath.'

Wise Men, shepherds, angels and such throng into the hallway as he continues. 'Ag, man! Our Christmas stables, woman, have offerings of whole hams - cooked and air-dried – Scottish and Irish smoked salmon, and Mr Heath's very famous pates. There's Coronation chicken, entire Stilton, Farmhouse Cheshire and Wensleydale cheeses, potato and artichoke pasties, five types of . . .'

'Les restes, cettes choses? Ha! Leftovers, bien sur!' scoffs the Comtesse Madeleine, a grande-dame who has flown in from her Loire chateau to be here. 'Roulade d'epinards with poached cucumber, quail eggs and aneth, ermm, what you call here, dill is it not? C'est ca? Vous etes fou!'

'Look, a pastry sarnie of Russian crab and fennel,' calls a ruddy cheeked veggie-stall trader, a swirl of sheets and tea towels, who's holding up one of my filo flyaways. 'Leftovers like what I ain't never seen the likes of before, luv. 'ave you?'

'Mine's Canadian lobster and Kent mango from Florida,' boasts the wiry, broken-nosed ex-boxer whose stall specialises in 'queer gear', tropical fruits and fennel bulbs and breadfruit and the like. He shudders his angel wings and looks heavenwards. 'Right 'ansome that is.' He bites extravagantly, showering shards of filo. 'And is that a touch of Thai lemongrass what is caressing me gob?'

'Proper quiche Lorraine here. No cheese, which is correct,' says a more serious voice. I give a thumbs up to uni-student Blake the Bike, who has cycled much of France to learn such culinary precision. Blake displays notable thigh and calf muscles under a brief mini skirt of frayed canvas strips. 'Best I can do as a Roman soldier,' he regretted when he arrived, play-thrusting a cardboard sword. Luciana assured him he had no need to apologise.

Feisty octogenarian Mrs Andrews pushes through, a St Trinian's nightmare in scarlet platform soles, fishnets, a shortened, pleated gymslip and untidy nun's wimple of fine curtain netting.

'I'm the future of that Bethlehem nonsense,' she says. 'This'll be the church in 21st century Portobello,' she giggles and then squares up to Miss K-T.

'What a sad and silly woman you are.' She pauses and I watch the summoning of her powers of deflating the pompous. 'I see you still eat too much. Never any leftovers in your house, I imagine.'

Long John Silver interrupts the laughter. 'No imagination needed to know that's right,' he mocks as he twists to accept the delight of his Magi mates.

Miss K-T's long career of insult, innuendo and bad manners is coming back to bite her on more than her substantial bum.

Jeremy puts up a buffering hand. 'And you are offering what?'

She smirks at the turn of focus and lifts novelty biscuits and chocolates, fancy tea tins and confectionery in festive wrapping, some associated with supermarkets.

Luciana leans to tower over her. It must feel like being mugged by a diamond-decked Statue of Liberty.

'You are at my door uninvited, for the wrong reason, and with no knowledge of fine food, however you spell fair,' she proclaims. 'And - a 'little' apology is never enough, I think. Sei d'accordo? Agree?'

Miss K-T is pale and wide-eyed with shock. She nods, her jaw aping that of a fluffy dog swinging in the back of a beat-up Cortina. Her lips quiver, too. I reckon it's not because they have a smart quip to throw.

'Trev caro, help this pazza leave the premises with her 'offerings' and ensure she doesn't come back,' Luciana orders, turning her back.

'Not helping that bag!' Trev protests. 'Been so bleeding rude about my coffee and anyways she got that Mrs Cheesecake to make Christmas mince pies for her. Didn't want to upset you, Boss, by telling. Not right that. Look there she is.'

In the spirit of New Year and today's Feast of the

Epiphany I invited Mrs Cheesecake, who is radiant at the sudden attention.

'Oh, then Mrs Cheesecake can help instead and also not bother to come back,' I say. 'That is not how Portobello traders treat one another.'

The applause from those who do not have their hands occupied with food and drink confirms this, but I expect there are many crossed fingers, literal and mental.

'Good word that, innit?' Trev says.

'What is?'

'Comeuppance.' He still snickers rodent-like, and I can't help copying. Luciana and Jeremy exchange glances not unlike scorn for delinquent children. Fair enough.

Oh dear, these shaming expulsions feel far too good but it's time to schmooze and to check everyone is here. And they are, costermongers, customers, dealers, suppliers, friends and others. From our Elgin Crescent and Portobello village are the hairdresser and his wife, the newspaper sellers, the toy shop owners, the chemists, the electricians, Mavis from Express Dairy and Fred and Tony the butchers. All except nervy Lena.

She's promised to come, and I called in on her a couple of days ago, but I'm not convinced she'll have the confidence without her late son Freddy.

Chapter 36

When Luciana and I answer the door again, my face is granite-like at the gall of more unrecognised and uninvited guests.

'It's me!' Lena laughs, taking pleasure at my frozen face.

I see it is, but Lena with careful, concealing makeup, her hair up, her heels high, a flashing Nativity star on the shoulder of her emerald-green coat and a very festive Frederick holding her elbow.

'You don't mind me bringing Freddy's dad along, do ya, love? We're in green because we is the shepherds' fields, innit darlin'?'

'Perfezione, brava, bravo,' says Luciana, guiding them in while showing little astonishment at Frederick's lime-green suit, purple shirt, white tie and pointy white patent-leather shoes.

'The purple is for them three king dudes, you dig me?'

Princess Luciana's aristo-ciety manners make a working-class, mixed-race couple as welcome and comfortable as an Establishment lord and lady. She steers Lena and Frederick towards Meredith, but it is Jem who is most welcoming.

The dynamic between him and his mother is discomforting.

Discovering its root is one thing I won't leave undone.

Meredith and Lena have called a truce. Lena's

chapped hands are the upper hand around here. Keeping a well-paid job brooks no such obstacles as public insult and despatch, so Meredith's offer of better pay and a bigger Christmas bonus won back Lena.

It's a challenge around here to find someone reliable to do your cleaning and polishing. On my deli floor problems with 'dailies' are as common overheard conversations as opinions about schools, what's on TV, which is the better Corsican resort and if smoking is bad for you or not.

At a nod from me, Trev steers the Four Must-GetTheirs from goading the sheep in the morning room and into the hallway. Luciana gathers Meredith, Jem, Lena and Frederick from a drawing room and pretending to want to show them something in the dining room is crossing the hall when a woman tumbles the last few steps of the darkened staircase, falls to the floor and lies stunned with crooked legs akimbo.

No-one can miss her gold-strapped high heels, the ones that were the secret of Luciana's Via Condotti carrier bag.

It's Helen but few know who she is or that she is faking.

Charlie ejects a high whimper and clings to George, burying her face and shivering. 'That's them, them,' she manages to tremble out, fluttering her arm behind her. 'They're the shoes Richard was wearing when he fell down your stairs, Nige.'

'Oh bummer, dude,' says Rupert.

'To the max,' agrees Nigel DB.'

'You sure, darling?' asks George, holding Charlie tighter as her head tips back and she falters. Both are cherubs, gorgeous in yards of floaty pink muslin, their skin and hair rubbed with gold dust. George pulls Charlie's head forward and Charlie darts another look at Helen's splayed feet.

'Hmmmm,' she breathes, as tears start.

'Tell me. Tell me how you know!' George demands. She shakes Charlie and would shake her harder. The glare of dozens of eyes stops her.

'See the sparkly little flowers on, on the, on the top straps? One came off and I kept it.'

'Bit ghoulish,' says Red, shuddering.

'She didn't know he was going to die, did she?' George snaps.

Charlie continues to mutter but it is hard to catch her drift. Luciana leans in and asks her to repeat her whispers. 'Well, it was so tiny most people wouldn't notice it, I thought. Am I in trouble, am I George?'

'Of course no-one would notice, darling! She didn't notice, did she? And she's wearing them!' George mocks, releasing an arm from Charlie and pointing at Helen's feet.

'They're Ferragamo, who cares,' mutters Helen, sitting up and still playing groggy. 'I told you that heel wasn't safe, didn't I, princess?'

Charlie wrenches herself from George and flapping like candy floss in a gale stands over Helen. 'You got them from her, that princess?' Then she whispers behind her hand 'George, George, what does it mean?

Is she the one, did she do something to Richard. Is she the one? Is the princess the bad one?'

With a predictable cry that she is freaking out, Charlie sinks to the floor. George waits until she's settled and then strides over her pink froth to confront Luciana. 'How did you get those? He was wearing them when we. . .'

'I borrowed them, from a shop in Westbourne Grove,' Luciana interrupts, grabbing the initiative by stepping closer to George.

'And thanks to your fairy friend on the floor there, we now know they are indeed what Richard wore. I wasn't sure before, so grazie per questo.

'When I spied strappy gold shoes with a high heel in one of those pretend boutiques off Westbourne Grove I was intrigued. Si, vero. You don't see a lot of Ferragamo in second hand shops, so I knew the shopgirl would remember where she got them.'

'People say anything these days,' Meredith blurts and turns away.

'She said was it was a woman with metal spectacles and an American accent.'

Meredith doesn't turn back but shouts over her shoulder. 'As I said, people say anything.'

A murmur of protest is building in the drawing rooms. The motley of Magi, shepherds, the bleating sheep and angels is pushed apart as Belinda steers Johnny through, using him as a battering ram to separate the tight host of stable guests. Yes, I do think there must be a ram/ewe joke there, but is it the time?

'And sometimes what they say is true, isn't it?'

Belinda demands. When Meredith continues to walk away, Belinda runs to grab her shoulder.

Johnny is stranded and confused, his tight-clung bible his refuge. 'It's not right, old boy, none of it is right,' Johnny mumbles. He licks a finger and struggles with it to find a page.

Helen has taken off the shoes. Belinda pulls Meredith towards her and snatches them from Helen's hands. She shoves them into Meredith's face.

'I saw you take them once and I made you give them back,' Belinda shouts. 'You must have taken them again when. . .'

Johnny moves faster than I expect possible and slams the open bible over her mouth but Belinda dashes it away.

'You had no respect for my son then and have none now. No respect for anything but a quick buck and a cheap thrill, Meredith. You used him. Alive and dead!'

Meredith's semi-permanent disdain slips. Is that fear I see in her cold eyes? If it is, she swerves. 'Used him? Him! He was El Portobello Cheapo, not me. Out for anything and anyone he could get, that one.'

I strike while her reserve is down. 'What, like you and labels?'

Meredith spins, puts a hand on a hip and laughs. 'What is this? The Inquisition? What does 'like you and labels' mean?'

'I reckon it means, where did you get this?'

I pull the Rahvis label out of my robe pocket and hold it high between my index fingers and thumbs.

Belinda and Johnny both stumble and Jeff jerks to support them. Belinda then stands as rigid as a rock, but I can't say if it is disbelief or something worse. Meredith tilts her head up and is feigning amused detachment, but I see fear flickering in her eyes.

'Isn't this the label from the dress Richard was wearing when you last saw him?'

Meredith tosses her hair and snorts. Belinda sidles closer to me and the label.

'Last saw him?' Belinda is having trouble speaking. 'Last saw him? When I last saw Richard . . . his red dress had a label. I remember the label was there. Was it this one . . .?'

She is interrupted by choking noises from Johnny. He is teetering and I wonder why his prostate cancer treatment is affecting him like this.

I take his arm and guide him onto a stack of bales in the tent. He won't let go of my robes and pulls me closer.

'She's a bad one that Merry. Heartless. Let me tell you.' He lets me go and falls back breathless. 'Heartless. It's not right – look.'

His index finger is in the pages of his bible and he shows me a quote with thick underlining. It's the quote Jeff discovered was behind one of the codes on my kitchen wall: Thy nakedness shall be uncovered, yea, thy shame shall be seen: I will take vengeance, and I will not meet thee as a man.'

I reel back but am saved from falling by the stout woollen barrier of the grazing sheep.

Does this mean Johnny wrote on my kitchen wall?

Chapter 37

It's too incredible that Johnny might be the anonymous scrawler in my kitchen, and I should probe further, yet I'm very conflicted because I want to get back to the Rahvis label. There's water, wine, fine Cognac and crackers beside Johnny, so I hurry back to the confrontation.

'Did I miss something?'

No-one answers. There's a stalemate of hatred and rage and neither Belinda nor Meredith knows how to proceed.

I reassure Belinda about Johnny, ask her again if she can identify the label. She's trembling so much she can't hold it steady, let alone read. Charlie and George take an arm each and guide her to a brighter pool of candlelight. Nigel DB and Rupert connect with the situation and stand close to deter others who are crabbing to see the label.

'It's got the right lettering, I think,' says Belinda.

'Thinking is not enough, Belinda,' Meredith shouts.

Strengthened by the defences of Charlie and George and the two lads, Belinda stands straighter. 'I have no interest in what you think!' She turns over the label and holds it closer to the candles.

'This is from his dress, that red dress. Look, there's a scrap of thread, a red thread, and that's the right red. (How did we miss that?) And a nick, look, as though it has been done too fast. I know when she took it.'

Luciana and Trev must be wondering with me how we lost time by missing those clues, when Johnny stumbles towards her.

'I do too, my love,' he booms. 'Remember? Meredith begged for a few last moments with him.' He reels forward, a tumbler of Cognac in one fist complementing the open bible in his other.

Holy Inspiration! In an instant I see what might have happened. Yes, I do know it's Robin who is supposed to say Holy Moly etc but no one can hear what is going on in my mind, can they?

'And where was that, where did Meredith rob the dead body of your son?' I ask.

'Yeah, I'd like to know that, too,' roars DI Harding elbowing his way forward as he tears off his tea-towel headdress and waves his badge. 'Oh yes and how did he get to the deli kitchen, anyway?'

From the depths of sorrow Belinda pleads. 'All I wanted was to make my boy safe and comfortable.'

'Then you shouldn't have slashed that bag,' says Trev. I could beat him senseless. Batman's Robin is supposed to follow, not lead. It's a dangerous diversion and nothing to do with what I have planned.

Long John Silver can't contain himself. 'I've seen her do that. Seen her. She slashes open rubbish bags to find out who has left them.'

'How could we know that?' whimpers Rupert the Red. He and Nigel DB are holding hands as tight as Charlie and George do, but for fear rather than love I expect.

'No-one could know that!' George adds. 'But if she did, then she's the murderer. Her own son on her own doorstep.'

The crowd's low mutterings of blame and opinion

fall silent. Belinda staggers and frames herself in the full fall of a sconce's candlelight. She lifts her face, speaking to a God she believes is listening.

'How could I know someone would dump my son on my doorstep – in yet another plastic bag. Another bag . . .'

'Anger at the bag, not the boy,' whispers Luciana. 'Remember I said that?'

I do and I choke up, imagining the moment Belinda realised what her slashing had done. I'd like to leave before the images get too strong and I expose my weakness. I am working on how I might when chef Lucca appears from the basement kitchen. He struggles with a silver tray mountain high with Dan's Deli sausage rolls which have become a local obsession even though nothing like the usual expectation. Perhaps that explains it.

These rolls are generous tubes of butter-rich pastry packed with my unique recipe of sweet-spiced pork with mint and dried apricots. It's a classic Middle Eastern combo with lamb but even with pork it's relevant to Christmas in my mind.

The aromas flood everyone's senses and erase all thoughts but of biting into a couple. Luciana senses the change of focus in the rooms and sees I also need recovery time. She threads her arm through DI Harding's as though a lifelong ally. 'We need space, don't we Detective Inspector?'

Before he can answer she is organising the guests. 'Those of you dying for a cigarette, please go down to the smoking room. Take bottles or glasses as you will. Lucca will show you the way and take sausage rolls. The rest of you clear out of the hall and then stay where you go. Subito, subito' she commands clapping her hands, which sends her jewels into paroxysms of scintillation.

Everyone obeys, like flocks of sheep with a snappy dog at their heels. Orlando is herding too, while ignoring Mary and glancing at Luciana for approval. She acknowledges him but there's no warmth in her eyes. Is her suspicion of Orlando catching up to mine?

In the hallway, the Four MustGetTheirs - Charlie, George and their boys - stand tight. I'm with Luciana, Trev and Jeremy. The shop's Blonde Beast Jeremy has been still and quiet and I realise that like many here, such scenes won't seem real. It's what they've experienced on screens or read about but they cannot connect with such events in real life.

Meredith continues to glare at Belinda and Johnny across the hallway but are they somehow united? By what? Fear of something yet to be revealed I expect. Fear of the truth, perhaps.

Jem stands with Lena and Frederick, looking fragile and alone. He's so much younger and I feel he's not coping. I'll remonstrate with Trev about his bag slash revelation another time. Right now, I remember our thought that Trev's the best one of us to connect with his Portobello generation. I turn him towards Jem and he understands at once. It's good to see Jem's appreciation of Trev's quick arm around his shoulder.

Belinda steps forward, holding up the label. 'You

haven't said where you found this, Dan?'

'Such a good question,' I say with great satisfaction. 'With such a good answer. I bought it. I bought it from Araminta, yes, Araminta, the woman who was murdered on Boxing Day.'

I'm understanding what writers mean when they say you can cut an atmosphere with a knife.

Rupert the Red is emboldened, I suspect because he realises anything to do with the label must have happened after they dumped Richard's body on his front doorstep.'

'Did Araminta cut it out of his dress?'

'No. But I know who did.' I pause then look at everyone present before turning to settle on Meredith. 'Araminta told me, told me who sold it to her. It was the same person who sold the shoes. You, Meredith!'

'She cut it out when he was dead?' Rupert shouts. 'Just to make a few bucks? Not cool, very freaking much not cool!'

There's no need to answer Rupert. Everyone turns to Meredith, but their unspoken intent is ambushed by gasps and sobbing intakes from Johnny.

Belinda is immobile and paling. 'Oh no! His heart. This'll be too much for him.'

'I've done first aid,' shouts Charlie. 'I'll look after him'. She rushes to Johnny whose face is claret red. He is slumping to the ground, too fat to fall flat. She's loosening his collar but stops with her finger on what I presume is his jugular.

'He's dead, George.'

'Don't tell me!' she huffs.

Chapter 38

DI Harding stops being a spectator. 'Party's over. Sorry Mrs Princess.'

'Princess is enough, DI Harding.'

'As you say, umm princess. Party's over.'

I'm thinking fast. The longer I keep people here, the more I might get clarity about Richard. Anyway, there's no way I'm having that food left. Leftover leftovers is not the plan.

Luciana acts again, pushing everyone else into the morning room and the dining room, where most of the food and wine is anyway. Luciana closes them off from the hall and shouts down to Lucca to bolt the downstairs door.

Belinda's crouching beside Johnny, holding his face in her hands and looking up at me. 'It was more than you know about, Dan,' she says. 'More than the testosterone and that. More than his heart and being overweight. The shock has been too much for him. It was too much, everything . . .

'Richard was killing him. He's killed him now. His son has killed him.'

She struggles to her feet and points at Meredith. 'But she's the poisonous one, the one with the final blow. Stealing the shoes and cutting out the label from a dress worn by our dead son. Her betrayal is what killed Johnny.'

Belinda takes a long breath, smooths her hands down her black velvet suit to straighten it and squares her shoulders. 'It can't harm Johnny anymore. And it is the truth, so I will tell you everything.'

Is she going to say the truth can't hurt? I hope not. It's the most untruthful thing I know, the crutch of cruel bigots.

Meredith moves as though hoping to escape downstairs. DI Harding catches Jeff's eye. The DS moves and holds Meredith's arm. She protests and he tightens his grip. For a moment I think she will spit in his face but she's too bright for that.

Charlie has retrieved a throw from a drawing room and covers Johnny's body and face.

'Oh, thank you, darling,' says Belinda. 'I don't know who you are but thank you. Were you all friends of Richard?'

'We were the ones who, who brought him home to you,' explains Nigel DB.

'I see, and I suppose you thought you were being kind to him.'

'We did,' says George. 'But now I, I see that we helped him die.'

'Yes. I must have killed my son by ripping at the bag with the knife.'

Like a stagey Lady MacBeth, Belinda walks around the hall in a trance, disconnected with reality, her voice low and her eyes unfocussed.

'Imagine my fury that someone would dump another bag late at night and then ring the bell to let me know. Can you imagine that?'

She stops and slaps her palms over her face, where they stay for many long silent minutes. Then she flings out her hands and staggers before stopping and pointing towards the ground.

Is she seeing the plastic bag before her?

'And then I see his face. And his eye. His eye caught mine.' Her body shudders and her head shakes. She pincers it between clenched fists and with that false stillness she faces us.

'How can I forget that single eye? Could you?' she demands, judging as she challenges each of us without mercy, one slow beat after the other.

'Was he alive, did he recognise you?' asks Charlie, breaking the tension. George slaps her and hearing this Belinda drops her fists and turns to them, coherent and attached to reality again.

'I'll never know. Or what he was thinking, if he was. What does a boy think or want to say when he knows his mother has slashed and stabbed him? Yes, I'll say it, is killing her son.'

Belinda opens her hands, pleading for an answer but none can meet her face or give an answer.

'What if he wanted to tell me something? Just like he always did when he came home, truths or not. No, he didn't speak, although I caught something in his eye, a faint glowing star, but it was so far away, deeper in space than you can imagine.'

I can imagine. I am living those moments with her but many more, too. No wonder she told Luciana and me she understood the suffering of whoever killed Richard.

It was self-pity.

My stomach is as cramped as if I have been stilettoed. Deep breathing isn't helping and the many different rhythms of weeping and sobbing in the room make it hard to keep steady and even.

'There was no-one in the street,' Belinda continues. 'No one in the shops. I managed to drag him inside but then, well, Johnny couldn't help. Who else would care, who would help Richard and help me?'

She pauses again, her focus once more turning inwards.

'And then I saw the star in his eye leaving. Not with a whoosh or in an arc across the sky, not like the gift of a shooting star, but a star starting a long voyage. It wasn't fading. Not dying. It was voyaging, yes, that's the right word, taking its light farther and farther away from me until there was nothing.'

A re-acceptance of this finality empowers Belinda.

'There was only Meredith. Meredith who I hoped loved him beyond using him.'

'Is this why she lent him dresses,' George asks, rude and unnecessary.

'Lent? No. She sold them to him. Encouraged him to wear them, just so she could take more money from him.'

'He got plenty back from me!' Meredith retorts.

'Your turn will come, Mrs Lopez,' DI Harding interrupts. 'Please hold your tongue.'

Then Harding rethinks.

'No. No it won't come, not here. Everyone will have to come to the station to make statements.

'Sergeant, get a couple cars up here, will you? Make that waggons, you'll all have to be there.'

'No,' says Belinda with determination. 'I'm saying it here, with witnesses.'

There is wide consensus and Harding doesn't protest when Luciana suggests we move to sit in the rear drawing room. It's cold in the hallway now but the fire will still be burning there.

'Yes, Johnny doesn't need to hear this again,' Belinda agrees with a sad glance at his shrouded body.

I've never been in this drawing room. Luciana's mixture of Italian and French décor is replaced with elegant English Regency furniture. A pair of scroll-ended daybeds is buttoned in pale jade-green silk brocade patterned with dragons and Chinese symbols for health and wealth. The dragons have five claws, meaning the fabric was woven for the emperor's personal household.

Formal chairs with their original horsehair upholstery stand in their correct place against the walls on double sabre legs and with crest rails and splats inlaid with fine brass designs.

Chapter 39

•

In traditional detective stories I would be the one making final revelations about Richard's death and pointing fingers. I'm absolved from this by Belinda's admissions and confirmation it was Meredith who took and sold the Ferragamos and the Rahvis label. Johnny's death has liberated Belinda from further concealment.

She chooses to stand, resting one hand on a Regency rosewood bonheur du jour. Ideal, I realise. These elegant small desks are where women sat daily to write their letters of gossip, intrigue and, sometimes, the truth.

'Meredith was the only person I knew with a car and somehow I thought that was important. She drove around and we managed to drag Richard up the steps, hoping he was still alive, trying our hardest not to hurt him and listening for the slightest sound. There were none.

'By the top of the stairs his body, we could, well, we knew he had lost control. We didn't know how much blood or anything else was in the bag, so we managed to get him into the bath and then we cut the bag away. Well, I did. Once I began, Meredith couldn't bear it.

'My beautiful boy was gone.'

No-one in the room is moving but Meredith, fiddling with the cross-stitching on her robe, crossing and uncrossing her legs. I empathise. She saw most of the same pitiful images.

'None of us knew what to do. I worried someone might think we had hit his head. Johnny didn't want funeral people to see Richard in a frock and high heels. It was tough enough in life for him but now it would be public. That was Johnny's worry.'

Even Meredith is weeping. Jeremy moves closer and lifts his arm to comfort her. Luciana stops that.

'Once he, Richard I mean, was in the bath he began to stiffen as you do. Meredith knew that would pass and, when it did, I washed him as though he were a baby. I powdered him and scented him, so he knew it was me, that I still loved him.

Belinda sighs. She can see Johnny's covered body through the half open door. 'Johnny, dear Johnny, couldn't bear these hours. Knowing Richard's body was in his bath was almost unbearable. He read his bible and reminded us that it was Carnival weekend, that there'd be plenty of people around if we did anything with the body.'

'That was a problem, lady.' Nigel is connecting more with the resonance of what they did.

'It was and we didn't want the police to know anything or to call an undertaker. What would they do to us, how could we explain that head wound. . . Meredith came up with the solution. She said we should take him somewhere neutral, where he would be taken care of but that had no connection with any of us. That's how she came up with the idea of the deli.'

'Why? Why there?' I spit.

'She said she wanted to fool the Deli-Detective. Didn't think you were clever enough to work it out, so we'd be safe.'

'That didn't work, did it?' George shouts.

Meredith is impassive but minute by minute looks smaller and more vulnerable.

'But why did you leave the dude in the frock?' asks Nigel D-B.

'Johnny hated that, too. But I knew this was important for Richard.

'Remember the Colosseum thing, Dan? Of Richard being a gladiator expecting to die? That dress and those heels and makeup were his challenge, his Portobello gladiator armour that put two fingers up to the mockers, the jealous mockers.

'Richard and I, we knew about history and heroes. Warriors were buried in the most splendid of their armour. I wanted him to go as a warrior. That's what he would have wanted I feel sure.'

'Others might see him as a pervert'.

Meredith's put down was met with astonishment and cries of mortification that strengthened Belinda.

'That's not how you saw him, was it, Meredith? You saw him as . . .'

'No, no!' It's Jem and he's screaming with his hands over his ears. 'She didn't, she didn't. I want to go away.'

Harding is perplexed. Overwrought children are not common in his patch. Meredith crosses to slap Jem and is raising her arm a second time when Frederick strong-arms her away.

Frederick holds Jem and I see tears glistening. 'I

was bad to my son, but I was always watching.' His dancing Caribbean vowels calm the room. 'I felt good, so good, when I saw Jem and Freddy together, so close.'

He gives a huge smile and kisses Jem on the top of his head.

'So alike you was. You could have been twins.'

The word ignites fireworks. Meredith and Jem both tear themselves away and stand rigid and confrontational in the middle of the room.

'I am,' Jem shouts. 'I am! I was born a twin, but she. . .'

'Don't be foolish!' Meredith raises a hand to Jem but Frederick swings him to safety, giving me a moment to calculate.

Is this true, was Jem a twin, and does that make him a single twin? Isn't there a word for that? I search for a phrase I can't quite catch. Then it's there. That's it. Bereaved. Is Jem a bereaved twin? If he is, that means he has a bereaved mother.

What dual volatility would that breed?

I sense doors opening in my mind, connections. Is this what Meredith meant when she said she would have lost everyone?

Luciana is decisive. It's too easy to forget how maternal this dominant woman is. 'Jem doesn't need to be any part of this,' she says. 'Trev, take him upstairs, first on the left, my boudoir. Stay there until Dan or I come up.'

It's agreed with DI Harding. It's a brilliant idea. I'm certain Jem has something to say but it must be said with minimal passion and pressure. And without his mother Meredith present.

When Jem and Trev are out of earshot, Harding asks Belinda if there is anything else.

Chapter 40

'I kept Richard as clean and tidy as I could. I'd done it when he was an infant and now, well, now he was just as helpless. The hardest part was that gaping. . . . his head wound. No mother wants to see her son's naked brain. I couldn't wash and dry his hair the way he would have wanted.'

The image is gaunt and I know most of us are seeing it too.

'I slept on the floor beside him the rest of that night and was with him as much as I could. Just talking, you know. As time went by it somehow became normal. The cold of this miserable winter meant time was kind to him. I kept the window open and there was no heating in the bathroom anyway. I made a more comfortable bed for myself the second night.

'We waited until the early morning after the big carnival day and Meredith came back with her car. By then Richard was supple again so it was easy to carry him. But, but . . .

'That was when Meredith exposed herself. Johnny came around and understood he had some need to show respect for his dead son. It was an awful struggle in every way, but he strapped Richard back into those heels, the final act of preparing him to leave us.

'Within minutes, Meredith took off his shoes saying she may as well have them back because he wouldn't get any more use from them. Richard might have paid for the dress, but she had lent him the shoes.

'Johnny protested and forced her to put them back on and do up the buckles again. She had negated his gesture and made him seem worthless. It was a stab to his heart. I think that's when he gave up his many fights to keep living.'

The room is stunned and looks to Meredith for justification. There's no reaction from her but a shrug, dramatising her detachment. The memory dumbs Belinda, so I change the subject, hoping she will strengthen.

'How did you get into my deli?'

'Meredith of course. She had the keys and the codes from Richard. Just in case he had said, and as it turned out . . .

'Once we were there the finality thumped into us, floored us. Johnny and I understood this was the end, that's what seeing Richard on the table meant. Once we left there, we would never see him again. It weighed on us like a ton but somehow we accepted it was goodbye and I was grateful I had had Richard for those extra days.

'Johnny found it harder. He became frantic about Richard's soul. He was struggling with saying goodbye to his son in a dress and with his strong feelings of wrath at all Richard had done, and why, well, why he was known as Golden Dick. We did know about his Secrets Tax and all that meant. And we're sorry we couldn't stop that.'

'He started to write a warning to others on the wall a memento mori that warned about the dangers of sin in this world. Meredith stopped him, saying his writing might be identified and would tell people it was us who left him there. So he wrote in that code.

'I didn't agree with Johnny's hatred. That's not what the bible means to me. So I copied what he did for my favourite bible quote - Hatred stirreth up strifes: but love covereth all sins.'

'You have to believe that,' she appeals, 'otherwise what are we doing here?

'We both said a prayer over Richard, and I prayed you would be kind to him, Dan. My last thing, the last I could do

for him was to freshen his lipstick and to scent him, so he would look nice and be nice for you, when you found him.

'Johnny left and that's when Meredith said she wanted a last few minutes.'

George breaks the spell. 'That's when the bitch stole from the body!'

Rupert steps forward. 'Didn't you see what she'd taken?' he demands.

'The weather was very cold, remember, and Meredith was wearing her ethnic layers. She could have hidden anything.'

'And then?' I ask.

'Then we went home,' says Belinda becoming more morose. 'Johnny and I sat up the rest of the night praying that Richard would have a happy ending.'

There's a question everyone in the room wants to ask., George leads. 'What about the knife and the sausage machine thing?'

Belinda's eyes widen with outrage. 'We knew nothing about them, nothing,' Belinda says.

The room's focus turns to Meredith.

'No,' says Belinda. 'It's true. She had time to steal the shoes and the label but not time to do that. That's one thing I cannot blame her for doing.'

'Unless she went back,' DI Harding suggests. There's another silence, deeper. Any movement in the room is eyes that enquire or accuse.

'Someone did,' says Frederick. 'Someone who hated Richard and wanted to hurt him even more.

'But who else knew he was there, that's a good question, isn't it Detective Inspector?'

Chapter 41

●

Trev tiptoes down the stairs and stands close to me. 'Boss, there's some stuff you'd better hear up there.'

'Just me?'

'I think it's best.' Luciana shoos me forward.

Jem is curled, foetal. Trev is massaging the top of his shoulders. 'It'll do you good, mate,' he assures Jem. 'And it won't go further than this room.'

Jem looks for guarantee in Trev's eyes rather than mine and then sits up but leans forward, his hands on his knees like an old man. He blows hard several times and shuffles his palms against one another.

'Well, it's about what happened on that Monday night,' he begins. 'Even though the streets were still crowded and there was so much extra light from boom-boom vans and food stalls, Freddy and I were out looking at stars. It got late, well after midnight. We went up Portobello, which was safer than taking a short cut.'

Jem pauses and I play my best detective strategy. I say nothing. Jem has no choice but continue.

'As we turned into Elgin Crescent, I saw my mother's car outside Dan's deli. We knew that was bad, that something was wrong and, well, to be honest, I was frightened about what my mother might be doing.'

'And what did that make you do?' I hope I am not being a bully, but I must make sure neither he nor I veer off and leave something unfinished. Jem is mute until he understands this is no longer an escape.

'So, I didn't say goodbye to Freddy like I said.'

He looks up expecting blame from me, perhaps anger at being lied to by him. I shrug it off and encouraged, he speaks faster.

'Instead, I asked him to come home with me. I thought the place wouldn't smell of pot so much if she was out. He'd be safer and I'd feel safer. But then, I didn't know . . .'

Jem scrunches up, his head almost between his knees. He repeats the phrase again and again.

'Know what, Jem?' I insist. Jem collapses, his thin body shaking. I stop Trev going to him. I want nothing to interfere with what I suspect is a confession – but about what?

At last, Jem straightens up, his eyes wet, his nose streaming. He wipes away the snot with the back of both hands.

'I didn't know the brownie Freddy picked up and ate was stuffed with, that it was a hash brownie!' he screams at me. His rage is so extreme Trev backs away.

Jem is reliving the moments, juggling his hands high and low as though forced to hold hot coals. 'He was allergic and started to choke and gasp for breath. I thought if I hit his back something would come out and he'd be alright. But he'd swallowed. He couldn't breathe, he couldn't breathe. And then he stopped breathing. I was holding him but he fell, dead.'

I'm seeing emotion and memories no teenager should know. Jem's face is scarlet as he holds back words, fighting not to say them.

'She killed him! She killed him,' he erupts.

I freeze. Trev has heard this before and we both agree with a look we must not seem to blame Jem. How can we do anything else? When Jem sees this, he is calmer but still pale with the shock of remembrance.

I feel all his pain. Yet this can't be about my excess empathy. I'm listening to a teenage boy who has seen the choking death of his best friend and who blames his mother for it. It's not the time to feel sorry for myself, so force myself to ask him what he did next.

'I couldn't lose him, not like, like Castor,' he stutters.

'Castor? Your brother?' The name confirms my suspicions.

Jem's head drops and his chest heaves until he straightens as though a load has been lifted.

'Yes, my twin brother.'

'So, your real name is Pollux?'

Jem flashes a look at Trev expecting laughter, but his face is impassive. Good boy, Robin.

'You can imagine what that was like when I started school.'

In an instant I see much more. I've got it.

'You're not Jem are you, you're Gem, with a G, Gem for Gemini?'

'Like that bleeding thing on his ceiling, the constellation, is it?' asks Trev.

'We made it together.'

'That's Castor behind the biggest star?'

'The only pic there was. My dad secretly gave it to me and I pasted it to the ceiling but almost hid it so no-one could see it and take it away.'

'Like your mother?'

'She wouldn't even let me call myself Gemini in case questions were asked. Jem was as far I was allowed to go.'

'How old was Castor when, when you lost him?'

'Almost a year.'

'How did you find out about him?'

'My father. He said she was holding us both but had been smoking pot. She stumbled on steps and dropped him – and he died.'

'So, you never knew him?'

'I can't remember a face. He's more a vague feeling I'm missing something I once had. He'd been beside me for almost two years if you count before we were born. I still feel him. . . but mostly I still smell him. He's something sweet and milky and powdery and – I can't bear babies around me.

'That's what was so great about Freddy. He wasn't a baby. It felt as though Castor had grown up and I had him back.'

'Sorry, Jem but I have to ask. How did you feel when you saw Freddy was dead?'

'I don't know the words but angry to the max. Anger I couldn't ever believe possible. I would have killed my mother and not cared. But then something more important happened.

'I decided I wasn't going to let her take another twin from me. She'd killed Castor and Freddy, but I wasn't going to be her victim again. Lose a twin again? No way.

'I wrapped him in carrier bags and an old sheet

before, well you know, he got niffy and then I put him in the freezer, the one in the basement. It's a big one, so I could lie him flat, with a pillow and everything. He looked like he was asleep. I could go and sit beside him and believe that, that he was asleep. We could do things together whenever we wanted, when he woke up.'

'So. No-one suffocated Freddy by blowing pot smoke in his face. No-one carried Freddy along Portobello Road'.

'No. He was always there. It was nice.'

'What about Freddy's mother, didn't you care how she was missing him?'

'I would have told her one day but I was there a lot, being a son to her. I thought if I told her, she'd take him away. The way it was, Freddy was mine forever, the way a twin should be.'

'Why didn't your mother find Freddy?'

'She didn't go there much. People say she dealt in old stuff but do that much because she didn't need to work. She had loads of money from an inheritance. She'd freeze old frocks because she hates moth balls and doesn't think they should be folded when they were frozen. My father's clothes were under them, lots of them. I put Freddy between them, so he was as comfy as possible. I knew she wouldn't touch them. She hated anything to do with my father'.

'Freddy couldn't stay there.'

'That's why I decided to send him to Castor.'

Trev and I lift eyebrows, not knowing what that meant.

'I remembered stories of funeral pyres of Greece and Rome warriors and what happens in India, too. Where bodies are burned so the smoke goes up. I wanted Freddy to become incense, holy smoke that goes up to the Gods. Then he could go up and be with Castor. They would both have someone at last.'

'If Freddy was your twin, he could be Castor's too. That's beautiful,' said Trev, putting and arm around Jem and showing an understanding of Jem's pain rooted in his own background.

'But you had to, you know, burn him' I say.

'I know but I had to think it was worth it. If I didn't, he'd never get to be with Castor. I did talk to him about it.'

The doorbell rings. The undertakers have arrived for Johnny. I stand at the top of the stairs watching Belinda as his bulk is managed over the porch and down the steps. She shivers and Luciana closes the door.

The police vans are there too. Harding has made no arrest on suspicion of anything but wants six of Luciana's guests to make statements. Charlie, George, Nigel DB and Rupert the Red are in one van. Meredith and Belinda refuse to travel together, so George is swapped with Meredith.

Luciana opens the doors to the morning room and dining room, instructing her housekeeper Elena to build up the fires and this encourages more drinking and eating.

When I can, I tell Luciana how Freddy died. She agrees it makes sense of Jem being last to leave the bonfire on November 5th. His plan to unite Freddy with Castor was doomed. Jem had neither of them in life and he had lost his dream of them being together in death.

No wonder he was weeping.

Chapter 42

I'm in the Cheese Cabin with Long John Silver picking over goats' milk cheeses. He's telling me things I do not know because I cannot eat them.

'Poor kid,' he says, noticing Jem has come in with Lena. 'Ignored and left on his own while his mother spent time and money on that wretched girlfriend I told you about.'

'Don't let him hear that.'

'It's got to be solved,' he says. 'And that knife on the body. Someone must have had a bloody big hate on to want to do something with that.'

I leave Long John and walk upstairs. He's forced me to get on with it. Who hated Richard so much? One person wanted revenge more than others in the litany Trev recites about the hordes Richard chucked to one side. It's too hard to pick one, because who knows what is lurking and rotting in another's mind? No wonder police give up.

Think about something else, I tell myself. That's the way to get the brain to do some sorting out and come up with a new angle. It works almost at once.

I remember the one other thing said about Meredith having a girlfriend. Mrs Andrew said it didn't have to be a girl.

The images in my mind race to an outrageous possibility. To unravel that tangle I need to know more about what Heather saw when she was waitressing at Julie's in Holland Park. I telephone her and arrange to meet for drinks.

'Not many times but they came there,' Heather confirms. 'Meredith spent heaps on her. Best wines, most expensive things on the menu.'

'Did you hear a name?'

'No. Heaps of 'dears' and 'darlings', that's all.'

'Which way?'

'From Meredith, nothing the other way.'

'Can you give me a description?'

'The other one? Quite tall. Blondish and always wore her hair up, rather 40s style. Clothes to match. Which included a hat, the way women always did then. Very much a part of that vintage vibe that's going on around here. There was always a veil down to the tip of her nose.'

Heather gulps at her glowing Campari and soda, unfocussed as she searches for more clues for me.

'Even so, even so, there was something about her eyes, even through the veil. They were brilliant but hard to tell if they were green or blue and her eyelashes were so black.'

I know who she is talking about but is there more Heather can tell me? 'Other people ever notice them?' I ask.

'They did! Customers and staff. Said how smart the girlfriend looked but were rather embarrassed at the way the older one would lean forward and kiss her so much.'

'Anything else?'

'My boss noticed how the girlfriend ate with her

elbows out. She said it was quite masculine for someone dressed so very feminine.'

'Might it have been a man in women's clothing.'

Heather stamps her glass down, throwing her head back.

'Of course! Now you mention it. Not a man, though. More a teenage boy. Beautiful skin and hands. Impeccable hands and varnished nails. Big hands for a woman but I was envious I can tell you. Yes, a man but more a boy than a man.'

Time to talk to Jem again.

'Of course, it was bloody Richard Metcalfe!' Jem blasts. 'That's why I kept saying she didn't have a girlfriend.'

Jem has jumped from his chair and is in my face. I am trying to be discreet, but he wants to tell it all.

'Why didn't you say so before?' I ask as I put a hand on his chest to stop him getting closer. He's spitting mad and it's hard not to wipe away his hot saliva.

'If I said anything she might have been worse to me. And anyway, if I said something how would I know if someone might ask more about Freddy and – you know.'

His point is well made, and I stop myself from identifying with his extreme frustration and sense of abandonment.

'Once Richard was dead, did she change?'

'For the worse, man. She smoked and drank like a mad woman. Whined even more about not having anyone. Not a husband or a daughter. So rude! She'd say that in front of me.'

I'm overloading with empathy but recognise this is selfish and change the subject.

'Hold on, where is your father?' I demand. Too direct, that's for sure, but it snaps Jem out of his mother-hate groove.

'Supposed to be in the States. Haven't heard for years. Soon after he told me about Castor, he went back, and we never heard again.'

'Your mother never explained?'

'She said he was a piece of shit and never wanted him mentioned again.'

It's irresistible. I go back to Jem's life with his mother.

'You must have felt very alone.'

'Not as lonely as when she started going out with Richard dressed up like that. Spending so much on him and leaving me to cook for myself.'

'Why would she do this?'

'Feeling sorry for herself. If she was lonely, she did it herself. No husband because she'd chucked him out – or something. Killed one of her twins and couldn't face the other one. Me! Then, because she couldn't have any more children, she never had the daughter she wanted.'

'So, Richard was a daughter, not a girlfriend!' He looks at me as though I have climbed from under a rotted log.

'Suppose that was why she thought it OK to kiss her so much in public. All that mattered to her was what went on in her own mind.' Jem stops talking and this time I feel keeping quiet won't encourage him. I resort to the ultimate shrink question.

'How did this make you feel?'

'I hated him, hated them both. I hated how my mother gave him so much and me so little!' His rage is total. 'She wouldn't let me remember Castor, not even to put his name on a birthday cake.'

He has stamped with every word. Exhausted he falls to the floor to sit cross-legged. 'Life had to be what she wanted, true or false. She never admitted she had murdered Castor.'

'Murder? That's a bit strong . . . '

'She murdered him, for sure, and that's one of the last things I remember my father saying to her.'

'Did anyone else know what happened?'

'My father said it was judged to be an accident, but he knew, he knew different. He was there. That's why he told her it was murder.'

'And then he disappeared.'

'Sometimes I wonder if she got rid of him.'

It's so unfair for a teenage boy to have such a burden. Yet in my perverse way I also sympathise with Meredith. She's killed a son and guilt affects how she treats the surviving twin. She's desperate for a daughter she can never have, and her husband is no longer around, whatever she thinks of him.

Not a good way to wake up every day.

On top of that, she loves Richard as a daughter but treats him as a doll, someone to dress up and play with. Now he's dead and she's alone again. Or is he dead because he abandoned her some way? Even if she didn't kill him, did she punish him in my kitchen just because he was dead? It seems typical for her to want a last, cruel, wounding word.

She's heartless. I've seen that. Entitled, too. When there is profit to be had she'll take it, even from her dead 'daughter'. But heartless doesn't mean she has no emotions. What if she is angry and hurt? What if she wants to punish Richard for leaving her by dying, unable to understand it was not his choice?

Did Meredith go back to the deli and want to punish Richard just because he's stopped being there for her? Then changed her mind. Does that explain the abandoned knife? It's possible.

Meredith had Richard's keys to my shop, so it must have been her, mustn't it? Except, could she work a sausage machine and would she know a Maharishi quote? That indicates a much younger person, doesn't it?

This new thought is pushed to one side, but that doesn't work. It's sticking there and I need facts to dismiss it or face it.

The solution is closer, but I can't discuss it with anyone else. I must be the Deli-Detective and work it out myself. No. That's wrong. The way to solve this is the way I began, by sharing with Luciana and Trev.

It's a sombre meeting. The shop is closed, and I have asked both to stay and come up. Considering what we have to sort out, I allow Trev a small glass of Palo Cortado, unsure if his palate will cope.

'More of the Portobello good stuff, Boss,' he says making me feel good.

'Right, even though you know I don't mind when

things are unsolved, I want to get this out of my mind.

'Did Meredith go back and punish Richard? She had the keys and the password. But who else did?'

'Anyone who ever worked here,' they chorus.

'We'll have to go through them again.'

'Except that would be people we know about.'

'There is someone we haven't thought about,' interrupts Luciana sounding apologetic, well, as much as she can. 'There is Lucca, my chef. You know he comes here to help in the kitchen.'

I didn't know that.

It's a rude reminder that although most recipes produced there are my creations, I have little to do with running the kitchen. I employ Rodolfo, a hypochondriac Italian (il mio fegato! blah blah) who is there part of each day and who organises the roster and I leave it at that, as long as good food comes up every day. Yes, I make bagels on Saturday but that's because there is so much else going on that morning.

The kitchen arrangements are not good enough, I see. I don't know who is on the premises or when, particularly from 6am when so much is done before we open.

'Lucca and Rodolfo make arrangements to suit themselves,' says Luciana. 'I know Lucca makes the pizza when Maria isn't here - and her lasagne and her meatballs.'

Trev leaps up and shakes his splayed fingers.

'Yes, and sausages.'

'E vero,' says Luciana, who remains quiet. I see her make a decision to share. 'There's one thing about

Lucca you should know. He's very bad with time.'

'Meaning?'

'He pays people to be where he should be, for the time it takes for him to turn up. He likes to sleep.'

'Even in your house?' Luciana shrugs, tilts her head and flickers her eyelids. I presume she means 'he's Italian' but think better of asking.

'Do we know who those substitute people are?' I ask, excited by this new lead.

'I might know some of them,' says Luciana with unmistakable reluctance.

Chapter 43

Frederick and Lena are well known around Portobello for being 'fixers' who will lend a hand to anyone for cash in their hands.

This morning they sit on my chesterfield with stiff arms and hands flat on their thighs. Jem throws himself into my bean bag, so I take a chair from the table and sit between them.

It's been easy to get the three here as Jem is allowed to live with Lena, where Frederick has also moved in. They go nowhere without him.

Trev is here as a stabiliser for Jem and stands in his eyeline.

'I see you wear a Maharishi badge,' I say to Frederick.

'Sure thing, man. I meditate twice a day. Lena's doing it too and look what a difference,' he says with pride. 'Keeps Jem calm too, the way Freddy said it would.'

That's the end of the niceties and I plough right in.

'Which of you knows Lucca, Luciana's chef?'

'We all does,' says Frederick. 'I help sort out problem things in his kitchen, Lena lends Elena a hand there when Luciana has a lot of guests.'

'What about downstairs here in my deli?'

'Well, sometimes I'd get a call and go to help down there.'

'Do I suppose this means you'd know about working the sausage machine?'

Frederick laughs. 'Oh man! Temperamental that

one. Had to sort it many times.' He leaps to his feet. 'Hey man, you ain't sayin' what it was me?'

'It's possible.'

'So is a black Jesus and Christmas in August, Mr Heath.' He sinks back, shaking his head, which he puts into his hands.

'And you, Lena?'

'What interest would I have in – well, what he said,' waving her hands in front of her as though I had broken foul wind.

'But you have keys. Or could get them,' I insist. She nods. 'Did Freddy know this?

'Oh yes. He loved being in a kitchen and thought he'd be a chef. Lucca gave him lessons sometimes.'

'In my kitchen?' She agrees again, this time more hesitant.

This is all new to me. There's a difficult silence. It's time to take a leap that might solve the knife and sausage machine mystery or will lose me all standing as the Deli-Detective.

'And what about you Jem? Do you know Lucca, have you ever worked in my kitchen, maybe with Freddy?'

He's startled and shrugs, glancing at Trev for re-assurance. Not good enough. It's time to be brutal, to do a Poirot and ask a question he won't expect.

'Have you told me everything that happened that night, Jem? You know, the last time you said you saw Freddy.'

Pale and scared he grabs my musquash rug and huddles almost invisible inside it. Frederick crashes on to the beanbag beside him. He puts his arm around Jem's furry bulk, so he becomes just a frightened face in a burrow.

'Get it out, man,' Frederick urges.

Jem wiggles deeper into the rug and beanbag. From inside his den he sniffs and snuffles. Without emerging he asks, 'What'll happen to me if I tell you something, something you don't know?' He's begging for forgiveness in advance but without telling his secrets how can we give it?

Trev must be able to see him. He crosses his heart and kisses his fingertips. Have to ask him where that came from, but it works.

'Something else did happen,' a hoarse whisper says. Then, encouraged that he has started, Jem twists out of the fur.

'When we saw my Mum's car, we didn't go straight home like I told you. We hid until she drove Richard's parents away. Then we went in to see what they had been doing. Freddy had keys because he had promised Lucca he'd get things going for him next morning.

'It made me so, so angry. Seeing Richard made to look so special and with that fresh lipstick and someone had sprayed him with perfume or something. I bet it was her. Even when he was dead, he was getting more attention than me when I was alive. I was sure she had done it. Typical. Him getting attention dead - never me alive!'

Lena and Frederick are electrified. Lena puts up a hand, to stop Jem. Frederick abandons him and leaps back to the chesterfield. She buries her face in his chest, listening but not looking.

'Freddy said I was stupid, stupid to be so angry about a dead body. I argued and said it was because I was so jealous of him when he was alive and that now I could show him what it was like to be treated like shit.

'I told Freddy my mother liked him like that in a dress and she treated him like daughter because that's what she wanted. She wanted a fake daughter but not me, her real son!'

The confession is getting too much for Jem. As it is for us all. Is he going to say what I suspect? He pauses and squeezes his chest with folded arms. He releases them with a hooting burst of breath. 'That's why I decided we would make him into one, to see if Richard liked being a real girl.'

Frederick pales under his dark skin. One hand protects Lena's ear that is not buried in him. The other wipes his face from forehead to chin.

'I was so angry. I just wanted to hurt him the way he had hurt me – even if he didn't know. The best part was it felt like I would be paying my mother back. It felt like I was allowed, entitled to do it.

'It started as a joke but once we started, I knew it wasn't. I wanted Richard to be a girl. But a dead one my mother couldn't spend time with. I thought I'd hurt her as much as she had hurt me. I wanted her to be angry.'

Jem lapses into thought, his shaking head suggesting images he's reliving but is reluctant to share.

'Freddy helped me get the sausage machine started but didn't want to help with, y'know, doing anything. So, he wrote on the wall, the way we saw other people had done. Didn't know what they meant but he guessed how they did it. I suppose he was saying you shouldn't mess with him and me.

'Then, when I had the knife in my hand, I saw people might think we had killed him, done that thing to his head. I was so spooked I dropped the knife. I pushed Freddy out so fast he couldn't turn off the sausage machine. We wore rubber kitchen gloves, so reckoned we hadn't left fingerprints.

'Freddy wiped the door handles and the keys and threw them down a drain and like I said we ran home and wanted to stay together and talk about it. We knew we'd been very close to doing something real bad.'

Jem is turning on the spot in the middle of the room with his eyes closed and his head thrown back. When he stops, he faces Lena and Frederick. If he continues the way I suspect he's about to do, it'll be the toughest speech any teenager has made.

'And when we got back, she killed him,' he explains, in a low but strong voice. 'My mother, I mean. She didn't drop Freddy and kill him like she killed Castor. She murdered Freddy with one of her hash brownies, even though she wasn't in the house. Freddy is the second twin she murdered and took away from me.'

It's the first time Lena and Frederick know how their son died. There's so much to absorb, both are, what's the expression - stunned as mullets? Or is it like stunned mullets?

I'm not sure Lena knows where she is. 'That damned marie-juana,' she blurts. 'That's what done him. And I can't even blame them Jamaican boys what live downstairs. Marie-juana and Meredith, that's what done Freddy. They done him.'

Lena repeats those last sentences, sometimes louder, sometimes softer. Will that help her absorb and understand?

'Anyone else know how Freddy died?' Frederick demands.

'Just us,' Trev confirms. Luciana too I remember, but say nothing.

'You tried to burn him on a bonfire,' Lena shouts. She erupts from the chesterfield and pummels Jem, who stands and takes it, as unmoving as a shop dummy. For a few seconds Frederick stands too, his fists bunched, and I fear he will do the same. Instead, he pulls Lena away.

'What did you do next?' asks Lena, sobbing with no tears. 'How did you treat my boy?' Frederick tilts up her chin and kisses both her wet eyes.

'Our boy, darlin', our boy.'

I make a decision I hope will be appreciated. I tell Jem to get back on the bean bag and settle Lena and Frederick on the chesterfield.

It'll be me who tells them how Jem treated Freddy.

Chapter 44

I relive and suffer every conflicted second of Jem's wish to keep Freddy close and keep him company. I explain the freezing and why putting him on the bonfire was Jem's hope Freddy would unite with Castor, his dead twin. Freddy would have a friend in the sky, somewhere Freddy would feel at home because he'd always loved stars.

Jem's twins would be together forever, even though he would be alone for as long as he was alive and could join them. I told them Jem had kept Freddy safe and close so they could continue to be friends, to be twins.

I'm in pieces, sodden with sweat and shedding tears enough for everyone in the room. There's pride here, too. I think it a good thing to save Jem the anguish of telling his story.

Once I have nothing more to say, he stands tall and straight.

'I'm sorry if I hurt you. I thought I did the right thing and I realise I was selfish. Thinking of what I wanted.'

He turns to Frederick. 'He was my twin. You saw that. I didn't want to lose him, because I loved him, loved him like I still love the brother my mother took from me.'

I'm awed by Jem. Teenage boys don't speak about love for another with such passion. Being a bereaved twin must make the survivor very different, hurting more, missing more and feeling more. Who but another bereaved twin could understand the passions that saturate Jem?

His speech has drained him. He still stands but his bony teenage body is trembling and uncertain as he fears what our reaction should be to his declaration of love for Freddy.

Jem, Lena and Frederick assess the feelings of one another without speaking. Each is sometimes disconnected from the room. Other times they stare, hoping to force an answer from the others' minds and mouths.

Often Lena and Frederick lock into joint focus, spotlighting on Jem. It's close to unbearable as I empathise with those two struggling to find the correct things to say and to do for a boy toeing the cusp of manhood, whose mother took their son from them and his twins from him.

Lena is first to crack. She mirrors what others have done, folding her arms tight and pushing her chin deep into her chest. As her head then rises, her face changes from distress to radiance.

'Love. I sees that I does,' she says. 'And from someone who never had a scerrick of it, that's real special.'

Frederick agrees, weeping tears even his huge hands cannot sweep away. He seizes Lena and pulls her up and they stand over Jem. It seems a threat and Jem folds, fainting I think, but Trev rushes to support him.

Frederick abandons Lena and swipes Trev away

before taking Jem by the shoulders and straightening him. Jem is terrified but he's held until he recovers and engages with Frederick. Every time his eyes wander or his head attempts to turn away Frederick follows, allowing no escape from his imprisonment.

There's a long solemn stillness before I hear Frederick choke as he attempts to speak and then grips Jem tighter. Does he want to crush him? I'd rather be witnessing the ultimate embrace of forgiveness. At last, Frederick catches his breath.

'Jem, you give our son Freddy friendship that others wouldn't do because he had a black father. You give him a brother, a man to belong to, that thing I never did. That can never be repaid, but by God I swear will spend the rest of my life trying to repay you.'

Group hugs are something I avoid but the one I see changes my crabby opinion. Love is everything my hippie past preaches and it's coming true. Yet, can love solve the dilemma the truth now creates? What if the truth gets out of this room?

If it does, what will happen to Jem?

I sense all are thinking the same when Trev breaks away and shouts. 'No worries! No worries!'

Batman wants to slap Robin with a very determined 'Ka-pow'. Worries are what we all have, worry about what will happen if this gets out. Worries that upright, righteous Frederick won't resist blabbing, that Lena will mourn too much in public and want to share her pain.

My great emerging fear is that Jem's young mind won't cope with what he has done, what he has seen, what he has lost. Who will hear his story then?

'No, no, listen,' Trev insists. 'You know why the DI had to take everyone to the station, don't you? They has to make a statement there, innit? This is how it works. A confession can be used in court only if it has been made on police premises.'

'What's your point? Jem and Freddy have nothing to do with that.' Perhaps I'm too testy.

'That is the point, boss. Just listen, will ya? The focus there was on Richard. Jem isn't suspected. He's not been mentioned, so won't be asked to make a statement. Even if he is, well, the person who could witness against him is, you know, not here.'

'Nothing the cops heard or overheard means nothing.'

'Anything!'

'Whatever you say, Boss.'

'That's right though. Jem says he waved goodbye to Freddy that night and that's that. He's not been asked to go to the station to swear that.'

Confusion is obvious, in Jem's face most of all. I summarise to clarify. When detectives asked Jem and Meredith about the Guy Fawkes dummy, they said they had no ideas. It was so easy for someone to hop over the fence from the shared park and replace the one he had made, using the clothes he'd laid out to use on the dummy.

Their story is an easy out for a sloppy detective who might not care much for a half-black teenager. Some won't see what's under their noses because it might make too much paperwork. They resist the truth, ignoring even the deep-freeze where Freddy the Fire rested for more than three months. It remains unsearched in the basement of Meredith and Jem's house.

What now? I can't think anyone wants to put Jem through much more. Trev must be thinking the same.

'How about I take Jem down for one of my mochaccinos. You make tea up here, boss.' They scarper as fast as I expect they might.

'I'm off, too,' says Frederick, his voice abrupt, cruel and harsh. 'Too much pain to live where my boy died. And don't you think I want to spend my life hearing you whining and moaning, lady. You'd be reliving his life every time you wake up or walk down the Portobello. That's no life for me.

'Me is off back down dat Jamaica way, woman. Pronto, pronto.'

'And me, what about me?' Frederick's reversion to idiom brings sharp focus to the barren future he predicts. Lena's voice is thinner than tissue and she's collapsed into a heap that's quite as fragile.

'I bin telling' ya what ya life will be, woman, you dig me?'

Frederick dismisses her with a gesture close to contempt and steps into the tunnel that encloses the stairs to the deli.

'There's one more ting,' he calls without turning. He treads down a few more steps. 'There's another ting, woman.'

His voice is sepulchral, funnelling at us from the stair-tunnel, chilling in spite of its dark resonance and lilt. I'm freaking out at his cruelty and I want to stop him but then I hear him again.

'Dat another ting is – well, woman, you could turn your back on misery and come wit' me.' He's now honey toned and I fill up as I hear his reason. 'Will you come? And, will you marry me, Lena, will you?'

Lena's hands fly to her mouth, blocking her repeated yelps of 'Yes, yes, yes, yes. Please yes.'

Frederick bounds back and smothers her. 'I'm sorry. Sorry I did it like that. I couldn't look at you, couldn't, in case you said no.'

'Fat chance, you daft bugger.'

Chapter 45

•

It's a week later. It's quiet downstairs in the deli and I am wrapped in my fur rug in the depths of the bean bag, with an early lunch of flaming-hot pizza and a goblet of red wine. It's an opportunity for serious thinking about writing a book of my food Gosh Factors. Nice idea.

The phone rings and yet again I curse for not having bought the extension cord I've promised myself for years. It's a struggle to get up and then get there without spilling or dropping yet hoping to answer it before the caller rings off.

It's Long Jong Silver, almost incoherent. He begs me to rush to Meredith and Jem's house, opposite his Garden Flat in Elgin Crescent.

'There's been screaming and police cars are coming from everywhere.'

It's still very cold yet Charlie, George and Jem are huddled on the porch, not arrested but doubtless being prevented from leaving by a circle of young constables. It seems cruel to keep them outside but perhaps it's just unthinking.

I'm asking if DS Jeff is there when he appears from the side of the house. 'You'd better see this,' he says, beckoning.

In the basement, there's a gaggle of forensics and a busy photographer around a long freezer, the sort you see in supermarkets. On the floor are two piles of defrosting clothes, full-length the way Meredith prefers. One is of vintage women's clothing and the other is modern menswear, most of it jackets and trousers.

'What's in there?' I ask, hoping there's no clue to Freddy the Fire's long stay in the freezer.

'A body. A man.'

'Can I see?'

There's no question in my mind. It must be Diego, Jem's missing father. Jeff confirms this. Jem has identified him.

'What happened?'

'You'd better ask them.'

Long John Silver interrupts with flasks of coffee he has scurried across the street, and they are shared. It was chance he was making cheese scones, he says. His reputation as a nosey parker makes this unbelievable but they are welcome. His big, rough scones are piled high on an oval blue and white serving dish, and each is pulled apart and buttered.

Oh dear. Even in this situation I am diverted by recognising scones as a good idea for the deli, a great way to use cheese leftovers. It's gratifying to see Long John has cut the dough into squares rather than pressing out circles. It's wrong that scones have become dainty. Scones began in frugal kitchens, a way to use soured milk and baking soda to make a fast bread equivalent, cut into portions with whatever was sharp and to hand. Even better, he pulled rather than cut the baked scones in half. So wrong to cut them because it crushes and smears the lightness of the baking.

Yep, Gosh Factors everywhere, even when a new body has been discovered.

Do I have a problem? Or do I have a book?

I've persuaded Jeff to bring Jem and the girls inside another room in the basement, which is a little warmer.

'We're pleased to see you,' says George, cupping a red mug in blue hands.

'Me, too' says Jem. 'I didn't know. I didn't . . .'

'Tell me from the start?'

'George has taken over the lease of Araminta's stall in the arcade and I'm going to run it,' Charlie offers.

'So, I thought they might like some of the stuff in the freezer,' says Jem.

'Are you allowed to give them away?'

'I'm not. I'm selling them. Got to. That's what they're there for and I need money. The Socials are happy I can look after myself here but there's not a lot of money. My mother didn't leave much I can get hold of, and I haven't heard from her.'

'And?'

'George thought it would be good to sell men's clothes too.'

There's a silence as three pair of troubled eyes drop.

Jem chooses to continue. 'Once we looked, we went deeper than, ummm, I had before.' His look pleads for silence. I comply.

'And then we found him. I knew it was my dad.' He's trying hard to keep his emotions to himself. The girls put an arm around him, and we are interrupted by DS Jeff.

'We're finished. You three'll have to come to the station to make statements.'

Later, Jeff brings me up to date. Diego has been stabbed many times and DI Harding is determined to charge Meredith with murder as well as preventing Richard's burial. But where is she? Discovering Diego's body increases the pressure on Notting Hill Police Station, but will Harding now pursue her with more enthusiasm?

We few who know the truth about Freddy's death don't want Harding to find her. We have no interest in Meredith being arrested for murdering her husband, because it might mean a new focus on Freddy and what happened after he died and that threatens Jem.

The other fall outs continue. Belinda has been charged with the manslaughter of her son Richard. Portobello is seething with discussion but finding no balance. Many have sympathy for her and how she must have felt as a mother when she realised what she'd done. Others are revolted by her keeping Richard's body at home and then putting it into my deli kitchen. That's the basis of a further charge against Belinda and Meredith, the prevention of burial. It's a serious charge with severe penalties.

The basis of this crime is that failing to give up a body can be associated with murder and the possibility of evidence being hidden. It's meant to be a deterrent, but how can it be when it's so little known?

Jem is stoic and shrugs off anyone's questions about how Freddy came to be on the bonfire, and it seems other enquiries have been shelved, including those about how Freddy died and where he was deep frozen.

I'm worried the discovery of Diego's body might suggest this was the freezer where Freddy was kept. So far, none of the detectives has 'done the maths'. Ha. Another mental diversion. Why do Americans say, 'do the math?' It's mathematics, not mathematic.

Yet, I know the truth about Jem and Freddy and now have a huge moral dilemma. Perhaps one of my biggest ever.

Jem should be charged with preventing the burial of a body. That would be right and satisfy my Caped Crusader mission to punish the bad. But this is Jem.

There's little sympathy in the police or the justice department for a criminal's past, little relief of punishment because of what might have caused his or her behaviour. His case won't be helped by the current battalions of righteous egotists saying, 'If it's the truth, it can't hurt you.' What a load!

Jem has suffered most of his life as a bereaved twin, knowing for some of this that his mother killed his brother. Her hash brownies killed Freddy. Now it seems she murdered his father, who was sympathetic to him. It's little wonder Meredith screamed she'd have no-one if she lost Jem.

Does he deserve to be punished for finding a soul mate in Freddy and wanting good things for him even when dead, no matter how twisted it might seem? He didn't hurt him and what he did do was for love. Even the dead boy's parents think so.

What would you do? Would you stay silent?

Or might it resolve itself some other way? The solution might be presenting itself.

With unintended irony, Freddy has been cremated and rather than Jem living alone in Elgin Crescent, he now sleeps in Freddy's bed with the ashes in a cardboard box beside him.

In a few months, on June 12th, Jem will be an 18-year-old Gemini adult. He's going to Jamaica with Frederick and Lena. He says he's looking forward to dead Freddy's new brothers and sisters coming along. I thought he hated the smell of babies.

Luciana isn't sure where her sympathies lie but hopes the change of scenery will contribute to his 'recovery therapy'. Trev is wistful and adds that the shock of blue seas, coconut palms and constant Caribbean sunshine should help quite a lot.

Richard Golden Dick Metcalfe and Freddy the Fire are nothing to do with me anymore. Portobello Road and Dan's Deli customers can blame or praise the Deli-Detective, but none will ever know the truth.

Batman and Robin can return to civvies.

You'll understand why I am entertaining a very greedy helping of satisfaction, because although so much has been wrapped up, there are still things to be unpacked.

Jeff and Heather have something to tell me, I'm sure. I saw the look they exchanged at the bottom of Luciana's staircase.

I don't know who killed Araminta but now that I remember Johnny saying Merry when he meant Meredith, I am wondering if Araminta was telling us who attacked her, rather than giving festive wishes. There's much 'of interest' to learn about the Man in Black and there's that worry about the situation between Orlando and Mary.

And why has Jeremy found blood splatters on the floor of the Cheese Cabin? Have I mentioned that?

Likewise, I've not yet solved the duck pate that doesn't taste of duck.

There are things left to do.

All very satisfying.

The End, but not quite. . .

Thank you . . .

Thank you for incisive reading, editing, suggestions, memories and insights to Father Anthony Parker in Delaware, my sister Faye in Waipu, Barry Nielsen in Sydney, Pete Howard in Brisbane, Andrew Smith in Toronto, Jeremy Freemantle in Prince Albert, Louella Hanbury-Tenison and Camilla Osborne in Cornwall, Carolyn Cavele, Sally Young, and Annabelle Louvros in London, and to the late Princess Luciana Pignatelli, whose friendship is greatly missed.

Coming soon:

THE DELI-DETECTIVE CUTS IT FINE

Who is making bloodstains in the Cheese Cabin?

Why don't the murders end when the Fat Lady sings?

Is Orlando who he says he is?

The Deli-Detective, Princess Luciana and Trev have their work cut out to stop more bloodshed on Portobello Road.

Read an extract on following pages here

And then:

THE DELI-DETECTIVE SNIFFS IT OUT

Extract from:
The Deli-Detective Cuts It Fine

Sliced open Spring 2024

Chapter 1

●

April 1979

Let's get it right, shall we? That hot-tasting fruit is chilli or chillies, spelled with two 'l's, as in hotter than Hell. The classic recipe dish is a chili, with or without meat, chili con carne or sin carne.

True chili dishes are seasoned with a compound of ground chilli, cumin, oregano, garlic and long-cooked sweetened onion. If not, it's not a chili. Some spice companies don't know their 'l's from their 'll's and pack powdered chilli but call it chili powder. Explains a lot of very hot and very bad chili dishes.

This is on my mind because a chili has been requested for a catered supper tonight, even though it is celebrating a singer, whom I thought would protect her throat from burning. I don't make a searing one anyway, but perhaps she knows the better way to eat chili, each mouthful taken with soured cream or something starchy, which helps prevent burning your internals and later disturbances. Just as every mouthful of curry should go down with an equal amount of rice and little or no beverage.

You knew that, didn't you?

My chili con carne differs because I stir in cocoa powder. It adds a mystic deepness that can be argued as almost genuine because chocolate is included in Mexico's complicated mole sauces. I serve chili with lime wedges, soured cream and blue-corn chips.

In case you are new here, I'm Dan Heath of Dan's Deli – A Farmers' Market Every Day. It's on Portobello Road, where a ribbon of antique and vintage traders springs to life every Saturday. I'm almost on the border between those dealers and the fresh fruit and vegetable stalls that run from Elgin Crescent towards the Westway flyover.

The singer I'm catering for is Wendy Carlisle, an Australian soprano of grand ambition that she interrupted by a scandalous relationship with an opera director when both were married to another. She's taken some years off the major opera stages, working instead in the smaller ones of the German and US State companies. Now she wants back into the Royal Opera or English National Opera and under the guidance of her manager Orlando Nowell-West is starting a quiet campaign with tonight's private recital.

Rather than producers and casting directors, Orlando has invited the cream of London's opera schools, singers on the rise who could be potential on-stage partners for Wendy. There are few other sopranos but tenors and baritones aplenty and a small growl of mezzo-sopranos. A future mutual coat-tailing is the presumption, I suppose, trusting that in opera a gross difference in size and age is no bar to an on-stage relationship of blood, body or dynastic ambition.

Wendy's difference is not that of most operatic sopranos. She only just fulfils the expectation of a Fat Lady who sings and then dies. She's not grossly overweight but is well-fleshed and at close to six-feet tall has bulk enough to create a notable chasm between herself and most tenors.

Tonight, Orlando and Wendy's objective is to get a buzz going, building a network of opinion that will be positive enough to get Wendy auditions or invitations.

Wendy is a long-time friend of my colleague La Principessa Luciana, an aristocratic Italian separated from a French prince. She discreetly deals in high-class jewellery from her perch at a counter beside the Cheese Cabin in my deli. Yes, we know she is properly la princesse, but La Principessa amuses her more as she has no wish for any association with her prince.

Luciana is also an excellent snitch, protecting the deli against shoplifters, smokers and such. This she does in concert with Jeremy, my South African deli manager, an ex-soldier and veldt trekker who wears khaki shorts and long socks whatever the weather. He is known to his staff as the Blonde Beast but in a good way.

Tonight's performance is somewhere I didn't mention in The Deli-Detective Wraps It Up. Princess Luciana lives in a splendid palazzino in Chepstow Villas, a street of cream-painted mansions that crosses Portobello Road at the top of the hill where Saturday's markets begin their entertaining melee of open-air stalls and dark arcades.

Where other houses have a garden or a conservatory behind them, Luciana's is built over with an imposing studio with cushion-panelled walls. One end is lit with a wall of Gothic windows, whose ecclesiastic effect is enhanced by the vaulted timber roof.

It's a splendid choice because it's both private and unknown. That means every invitation has been accepted and the recital will be spoken of in the right circles tomorrow. I've learned on the deli floor that restricted privilege is a great creator of gossip.

The 25 guests include me and the princess, Jeremy, Mary from the deli floor who is half Orlando's age but seems to be having an affair with him, plus my friends Helen and Jeff, both of whom are keen opera goers. Helen and I bonded during our cancer treatments and Jeff is a detective sergeant at Notting Hill station on Ladbroke Grove. He has informally helped me solve some of the crimes that led to me being christened the Deli-Detective.

Chapter 2

Luciana is unhappy because the recital is late starting. She's not the hostess even though she's the best dressed here, but it's her studio and she wants all to go well. Luciana is in smoky pink crepe that hovers close to the body from her throat to the floor without interruption by defined waistline. It seems suspended from a bib-style gold necklace that's studded with primary-coloured cabochon gemstones.

'It's Bulgari,' she told me. 'Although I understand why some say Vulgari.'

Luciana looks more a prima donna than Wendy, her hair newly blonded and sculpted to hide even hairline scars from the pioneering scalpel of Brazilian Pitanguy. She's fiddling with her necklace as she asks, 'So how long do you think?'

The soprano has developed stage fright. Pale, clammy and struggling to breathe, she's still in a dressing gown, resting with Orlando holding her hand at one end of the makeshift kitchen attached to the studio. From time to time, I see him refreshing the cologne on her handkerchief. He must be using too much because it makes her cough and struggle more.

I'm there too because I'm ensuring all will be ready for the later fork supper but can't help wondering if Wendy should not be warming her voice. When I ask, Orlando dismisses the idea. 'A diva is always ready.'

'Well, then,' says Luciana. 'She'd better get on with

it, Mr West. Subito, I suggest. Very subito.'

'That's Nowell-West,' he corrects, but has turned his back so Luciana doesn't hear him. Oh? The hyphen must be very important to him.

Spindle-legged gold chairs and small round tables that seat four have been hired. They sit unsteadily on oriental carpets over lifting parquet floor tiles. There's candlelight from brass wall scones and a scintillating chandelier dripping with crystal drops cut like icicles. There's a dais at the end opposite the windows and here Wendy will be accompanied by a boudoir grand piano, something smaller than a grand and just bigger than half a concert grand.

I worried the pair of triple-branched candelabra on the piano looked like refugees from a Liberace stage set but Luciana dismissed that. 'I doubt his were Regency neo-classical silver by Paul Storr.'

'Paul Storr?'

'The Prince Regent's favourite silversmith, but you knew that,' says Luciana turning away. She is mocking me, but we are both smiling because she knows I know. It's the sort of thing you absorb on Portobello Rd. Ah, forgot to say. Long John Silver is also here, a young rubber-limbed silver dealer who seems to know many of the guests.

Luciana's live-in chef Lucca and housekeeper Elena are serving Codorniu cava, a sparkler from Spain in matte-black bottles that I've introduced with great success. It's lighter and sharper than champagne, the perfect partner to miniature versions of my signature flyaway filo pastry squares, this time stuffed with poached cucumber and smoked salmon pate, about which we'll chat some other time. At this size the razor-thin pastry shards created with each bite are minimal but would still be enough to fuss Trev, the deli's neatnik barista. He's not here, refusing to listen to that 'stupid screaming'.

Wendy floats in wearing rather a lot of eau-de-Nil silk, encircled with layers of wispy panels. Are those real emeralds at her wrist, throat, ears and in a clip in her Irish red hair? If so, I expect they'll be lent by Princess Luciana, from the vault in her dressing room.

Wendy signals her pianist but Orlando steps forward with two raised hands. He demands the violet velvet curtains that hang ceiling to floor either side of the windows are drawn, saying that street lighting is detracting from the atmosphere, weakening the candlelight. There might be traffic and passersby, too.

The curtains are heavy because they are lined and interlined. It takes time, enough for me to walk through with more cava and chat to some of the guests. You never know where a new client might lurk.

Wendy is heaving with breathlessness and dabbing her shiny forehead and decolletage with the cologne-scented handkerchief. She's looking paler in my view but once Orlando signs he is happy, Wendy steps on to the low dais.

Her voice quavers as she says she will vary the printed programme and begins with what she claims is her most famous aria. I know it as One Fine Day, from Puccini's Madame Butterfly. She introduces it as Una Bella Giornata from Madama Butterfly. Its wrenching message of hope suits her pallor and fragile voice so well I forget she's unwell and ill-prepared.

She begins another solemn aria, this time from La Boheme, the one with the heart-tugging line about parting senza rancor, but she chokes halfway through. She's grabbing her throat and inhaling with difficulty. She leans heavily against the piano, her handkerchief to her mouth, and rasps as she tries to get air.

Frightened, confused by what is happening, she flails and then falls, almost disappearing in a flutter of silk panels. There is a knowing rustle of concern in the room for the state of her throat.

Orlando and the pianist help Wendy to her feet and there are agitated sotto voce conversations. She is deposited on a couple of golden chairs and fanned with parchment-paper programmes. They don't help much.

Will she be able to continue? It's selfish but Luciana and I don't want the event to be wasted or to be left with leftovers. There's more than the chili. There's lime-infused pasta salad with prawns and my pork, apricot and mint sausage rolls. Individual Pavlovas too, marshmallow centred meringues with whipped cream scented with orange-flower-water and topped with roasted peach slices. I'd like a pound-note for every chef and food writer I've had to tell that crisp meringue is not a Pavlova and that the texture is right only if vinegar is added to the whipped egg whites.

'Do you think someone else would like to sing in

the meantime?' I whisper to Luciana. She laughs but keeps it discreet. 'They all will, caro, any chance to outdo the others.'

'How would you choose?'

'It would be tricky, perhaps impossibile. They could only do the music the pianist has and so few of them are sopranos.'

'Not necessarily a problem,' interrupts Jeff.

'How does that help?' I ask, exasperated because I can't understand what he means.

'Wait,' he says with a smile. He takes Orlando and the pianist aside and I see they agree about something. Jeff bends to talk to Wendy. Her eyes widen but then she waves a limp hand, as if she were dying on stage.

Orlando claps for attention. 'Our prima donna, our dear Wendy, is temporarily unable to continue.

'However, the diva has graciously agreed that while indisposed the evening of arias may continue with the programme she had chosen.' The protests are loud but followed by chatter speculating who might take her place.

'And that's what will happen,' Jeff announces. With no explanation he asks, 'Could you do supper now, Dan? I'll need 30 minutes.'

I agree, he asks Luciana permission and then disappears back into the house, taking the accompanist and the sheet music with him.

Orlando and Mary help with serving. It's bitchy of me, but I reckon, they are hoping the guests think they are Princess Luciana's little helpers rather than mine. I hear Orlando suggesting Wendy might well recover, encouraging everyone to stay. There's keen wonderment table to table about whom Jeff will have gathered at such short notice if Wendy cannot continue.

Just as the Pavlovas are served Jeff returns and steps onto the dais with the accompanist, who arranges the sheet music in place. The guests turn to the door he came through, expecting an arrival.

Instead, Jeff plunges into Mozart's, Queen of the Night aria from The Magic Flute. It features the highest coloratura notes in opera as the inflamed Queen shoves a knife into the hands of her daughter Pamina and demands she kills the sorcerer Sarastro or be banished.

I'm so startled I half stand. How can my friend Jeff, a well-built detective bloke, sing like that? I didn't know it was possible for any man. Luciana forces me back into my chair.

'Countertenor, or what church choirs called falsettists before castrati came along,' she whispers.

'What's a castrati?'

'I'm cutting you off. Be quiet!'

Whatever it's called, I've never heard anything like this in real life. From Radio 3 I now recall the light sweet voice of Alfred Deller and the more robust sound of James Bowman, but seeing a man do this in front of me is confronting and I have to stop myself from giggling. I suppose it's the same shock that makes people laugh when they discover someone dead. The brain has no experience or language to cope, so engages a default.

With my eyes closed I'd be pushed to identify it as a man or a woman singing but there's no doubting the musicality, the accuracy and occasional great beauty. There's nothing of the self-deceiving Florence Foster Jenkins about Jeff's performance but a sense of purity, yes and of soaring in great spaces that makes me think of cathedrals. Yes, I think, it's that loud. How does he do it?

Jeff delivers much of what Wendy promised but adds astonishing virtuoso pieces I recognise as baroque, even though I know none of them.

It seems effortless as Jeff projects the poignancy and drama behind each piece, varying his tone and attack with such finesse there's awed silence after each aria, punctuated only by Wendy's battle to breathe. Orlando takes her arm to help her out of the room, but she refuses.

Jeff announces he will end unaccompanied, and the pianist is clapped off the stage. Jeff gives us Dido's Lament from Purcell's Dido and Aeneas. No trills or runs, no sky-high notes, just pathos, beauty and Dido's regret that Aeneas 'once had thought of leaving me '.

This time the applause is thunderous and feet stamp, the way they do at the Proms in the Royal Albert Hall.

Wendy is not clapping and as more realise this the noise falters. Wendy turns her torso to the audience, her face expressionless and white. Is she angry at Jeff's success or is she confused and thinking the adulation is for her? I think it's the latter but then she tips sideways onto the floor and makes a desperate gasp for air followed by silence.

It's not a classic death rattle because the air is sucked in but we don't hear it come back.

Orlando mewls like an abandoned kitten. He drops to his knees with a thump, waves her handkerchief under her nose and then pulls back the emerald bracelet to feel for a pulse.

The room is hushed and unmoving as Orlando places her arm across her breast and then feels the jugular in her neck.

'Morta. La diva e morta,' he pronounces, bowing his head. He stands and inscribes an exaggerated sign of the cross over his chest. Then he pulls out a jewelled crucifix, kisses it, and places it over her breast.

The poignant last words of Jeff's final aria swirl around my brain: Remember me, remember me, but ah! forget my fate.

I already suspect I won't be able to forget Wendy's fate.

'I'll get my emeralds,' Luciana says.

Chapter 3

DS Jeff is quick to take charge. He's checked Wendy is indeed dead and moves everyone who is crowding the body. Some have been praying over her as they knelt.

'No-one can leave, of course, but there's no need for them to stay in the studio. Can they go up into your house, princess?'

Elena and Lucca guide the guests out, leaving only Luciana, me and Orlando with Jeff.

'You'll have to call DI Harding,' I say to Jeff.

'I will but I thought it might be useful for us to think about what's truly happened. I mean, is this a natural death or . . .'

'It's premature but I expected it,' Orlando sobs. 'She's not been well for some time. Nerves you know and her heart.' He's whimpering but an unsympathetic glare from Luciana ends this.

'Why was she putting herself through this?' she demands.

'Ambition.'

'Never quite enough, I feel,' says Luciana with a dismissive wave. 'Was she usually this uncertain before singing?'

'Stage fright, nothing unusual. I was teaching her to think of it as excitement.'

'Don't nervous performers take tranquillisers these days?'

'We agreed nothing artificial in her body, nothing

but pure and natural.'

Luciana lifts an eyebrow. She thrives on everything artificial and unnatural that's offered.

'Doesn't seem to have worked, non e vero?'

I'm suspecting this is not a natural death. Wendy's stage fright seemed more like stage fear, and I can't wait to share my thoughts with Luciana.

'I'd better take my emeralds,' Luciana says, leaning forward. Jeff catches her arm. 'Not yet, princess, you know that.'

Luciana purses her lips but then sniffs a couple of times, well, not sniffs but the slow, deep breaths a connoisseur takes when their nose is deep in a glass of wine. Her jaw works as she rolls the scent over her palate, trying to solve a puzzle she hasn't shared.

'Very curious,' she murmurs.

'What is?'

'Not sure. They use strange substances on fabrics these days, to give body, but this is something familiar.'

'May I?' Jeff agrees and I lean forward also to sniff. I take longer than Luciana because the cologne Wendy used remains overpowering, and I'm finding it hard to separate out any other scent I can be certain about.

'Did Wendy smoke? Was that her problem?' I ask as I straighten.

Orlando is outraged. 'She's a soprano! That's why smoking was forbidden in here tonight.' Then he sobs and covers his face. 'I'm sorry, sorry, sorry, diva. You were a soprano.'

'So was my late friend the diva assoluta Maria Callas,' Luciana snaps. 'She smoked.'

Jeff's boss DI Harding arrives with a photographer, a forensic officer and clutch of constables, some of whom are sent up to ensure no escapees. They'll all have to be questioned.

The investigator dislikes the strength of Wendy's cologne and holds a handkerchief to his mask. I'm not surprised to see him use a torch to examine Wendy's nasal passages and then her throat. He mumbles as he reaches for fine pincers and then takes a moth from the back of Wendy's throat.

Orlando cries out and pushes his fist into his mouth 'A moth has choked her!' When he sees two more moths taken from her throat he spins away, a palm flat to his forehead.

'It was I! I who killed her!' he sobs. He turns and points at the curtains. 'It was I. I and the curtains, we did it.'

'Shouldn't that be 'it was me'?' I ask Luciana. Foreigners always know better.

'Of course it should,' Luciana agrees, shaking her head. 'It was I' is pedante, pedantic. Old fashioned. You might as well say thou.'

I can't help it. 'Thou seemeth a bit over wrought, Orlando.'

He didn't get it. I stopped myself from saying 'even for thou'.

'I wanted everything perfect for Wendy, but I should have left them,' he says. Luciana is furious. 'Left or not, my curtains do not hold moths.' Orlando shrugs and turns to look down at Wendy, crossing himself again.

'Those curtains do seem likely,' says the Forensic Officer. 'That's all I can say for the moment.'

'Basta with your moment, officer! Offensivo. Sono insultato! Il mie tende, my curtains, do not have moths.' She leans on his shoulder and bends over Wendy. 'Would you kindly shine your torch on the bracelet? Move it a little, per favore.'

Luciana directs the torch from the bracelet to the necklace, the earrings and to the hair ornament, her facing getting darker. What might she discover that I did not? Nothing to do with smell, I suspect.

She stands and her eyes are glittering, although with rage or triumph I cannot tell. 'I understand why you won't let me touch my emeralds,' she says, with great calm, warning me something bad is to come.

'And I presume you allowed Orlando to remove his crucifix because he placed it there after Wendy died?'

Jeff is perplexed, shrugging his shoulders at me. I hadn't noticed it gone and turn to Orlando. He takes it from an inner pocket, saying, 'That's right. That's what I thought. Didn't want it to be confusing.'

'But let me tell you something, amici miei, shall I?' Luciana continues, striding towards the direct light of a sconce. 'That is not my bracelet. Those are not emeralds. They are finto, falso, fasulli. Fake, fake, fake. Worthless!'

It's doubtless the wrong time but I ask anyway because I bet it's in everyone else's thoughts. 'If that's worthless, Luciana, how much is the real stuff worth?'

She doesn't mind.

'Tens of thousands. More if I can prove Empress Eugenie brought them to Paris when she married Napoleon III. She died here, you know? They both did.'

'Another bloody French revolution?'

'Bloodless, but mine will boil with sangue if my emeralds are not found and returned. Your move, Mr Harding.'

DI Harding orders a constable to do nothing but guard the remaining jewels until they are removed and put into a police safe as evidence.

Luciana takes out a gold pencil and a miniature notebook of ivory sheets. The young officer blushes as she leans in and copies down his name and number.

'I won't forget you, young man.'

'I couldn't forget you,' he mumbles between very tight lips. Luciana is flustered and none of us dares meet her eye. Is the PC flirting or threatening?

She continues her relentless pursuit of ensuring proper follow-up, something Notting Hill police are not famed for doing.

'You are in charge Mr Detective Harding. I know whom to sue if they sparire, if they disappear from police custody.

'And, Mr Harding, your man on the floor there must be very careful with the falene, those moths.'

'How's that, princess?'

'They are also evidence of, how do you say - of ill-doing.'

'Say again?'

'The moths could not have come from this room. Only the curtains are of cloth in here and I specified artificial fabrics, all of them, the velvet, the lining and the backing.'

'Seems to have been the right decision,' I say.

'Not for the killer.'

To be continued. . .

Glynn Christian

In the 1970s Glynn Christian changed the UK's world of delicatessen and specialty ingredients with MR CHRISTIAN'S Provisions, opened in Portobello Road market, and is honoured with a Lifetime Achievement Award from the Guild of Fine Foods.

He pioneered modern TV cookery on BBC Breakfast Time three times weekly and helped found both the Guild of Food Writers and the Great Taste Awards. He was the first Food Editor of ELLE UK and wrote weekly for The Sunday Telegraph.

The author of many cookery books, his special interest is ingredients; REAL FLAVOURS was voted best food guide in the world and the updated version is TASTE! How to Choose the Best Deli Ingredients. This and Basic Basics 350+ KITCHEN HACKS & HINTS were published by Grub Street in 2021.

His books about his ancestor Fletcher Christian, leader of the 1789 mutiny on HMAV BOUNTY, have been definitive works of reference since 1982. They include FRAGILE PARADISE, MRS CHRISTIAN – BOUNTY MUTINEER (historical fiction) and in 2021 THE TRUTH ABOUT the MUTINY on HMAV BOUNTY – and the FATE of FLETCHER CHRISTIAN (Pen & Sword)

Printed in Great Britain
by Amazon

27314304R00165